OTTO'S BLI

By Leo Ke

OTTO STAHL – BOOK 2

This Edition Edited and Published by Benchmark
Publishing
Bootham, York, England
www.benjaminlindley.co.uk

First Published Worldwide in 2017

'If the British told and enjoyed and embroidered some versions of the truth, they did so because that helped them to stay in the war. Like the veterans of Dunkirk itself, they did the best they could with the weapons they had, and they survived to fight again. That was enough. The truth cannot hurt them now.'

Dunkirk: The Necessary Myth
N. Harman

AUTHOR'S NOTE

The reception of the first part of Otto Stahl's memoirs has been very gratifying for me as an author. For Herr Stahl himself it has been rather lucrative too; but then he is a businessman and for him (as he puts it) 'the rouble can't roll quick enough'.

Readers of all ages have written to me, expressing their interest in one way or other. There have been the usual schoolboys wanting to 'do' Otto's life for their 'O' levels; several maiden ladies, obviously with hope still blossoming in their virginal bodies, desiring signed photographs of 'dear Mr Stahl'; and eager fans preparing to 'play war games with Hauptmann Stahl'. Hauptmann Stahl's reply to that particular offer is unprintable.

Of course there have been crank letters too. 'Don't you dare come to Wigan, you arrogant square-headed sod... signed anonymous' is their general tone. I can tell 'signed anonymous' here and now that Otto has no intention of sullying the holy soil of Wigan with his presence, not even if he were asked to do a signing session of his book at the local W. H. Smith's. No way!

A few of the readers' letters have been critical, mainly about the accuracy of Otto's recollections after such a length of time. Of course, some of Otto's statements about his experiences do sound quite outrageous, I can appreciate that, and a biographer like myself has to spend a great deal of time trying to verify the facts, in spite of Otto's oft-reiterated statement that, 'I've never told a lie in all my life, well, not often.'

For this present volume, I can assure the interested reader, that I have taken extra care to check the details of Otto's experiences in England and on the Continent. I have been able to verify that two German civilians were captured in a commando raid on the French coast immediately after Dunkirk, though it was not the first commando raid as Otto maintains. That honour goes to a group which missed its target, France, landed by mistake in German-occupied Jersey and returned with three punnets of strawberries and several pounds of tomatoes as their war-booty.

I have also been able to confirm by reference to the newspapers of the period held at the Newspaper Museum in Dortmund that an unnamed German civilian did escape from the temporary POW camp at York Racecourse in the winter of 1941. So Oberleutnant von Werra was not the only German to escape from a British camp in World War Two.

'Of course, it was me who yer read about,' Otto said when I informed him of my find. 'But naturally, von Werra was an officer and a gentleman and he had this little lion cub, which looked bloody good on the front cover of the mags. That's why they played him up, the shits!'

As the reader can see, Otto has not lost his taste for earthy language. I have even been able to confirm that there was one 'Alf Cheetham, employed as a caretaker at HM Embassy in Athens during the German invasion of that country. Unfortunately he has long passed away, apparently due to drink.

It is quite clear to me, of course, on what score most of the complaints about this second volume of Herr Stahl's memoirs will come: the business of Mr Winston Churchill's illegitimate son, the Hon Reggie Gore-Browne – "Kicked out of Harrow – buggery! Sent down from Balliol – Indecent exposure! Sacked from the Foreign Office – Importuning in Hyde Park" (as, according to Otto, Mr Churchill once described his son). As a loyal admirer of the Great Man myself, I undoubtedly would feel the same indignation at Otto's revelations, if I didn't believe in them implicitly, which I do.

Naturally a lot of older readers will be familiar with the insidious rumour that circulated during World War Two that the bespectacled, moon-faced Mr Brendan Bracken, who appeared from obscurity to become Minister of Information in Churchill's wartime cabinet, was Mr Churchill's natural son. But I doubt if even they will accept the Hon Reggie Gore-Browne.

I have made the point to Otto. But he sticks doggedly to his story. In reply to my most recent letter to him on the subject, he sent me a photograph of two white-haired elderly gentlemen with bronzed faces sitting under a palm tree. Turning it over, these words were clearly visible: 'Love and kisses to Otto, from his chums Rodney and Reggie, Marrakesh, 1979'.

In his own hand, Otto had scribbled in pencil, "The best I can do for you, Leo. Don't bother me again until you get the shekels from the new book. Otto."

Leo Kessler, Denia, Spain, 1981

BOOK 1 – IN THE BAG

CHAPTER 1

'Otto,' the Count said, ignoring the noise coming from the waiting men.

Otto Stahl took his gaze off the lone Heinkel III limping low over the French countryside, its port engine silent, trailing a plume of black smoke behind it through the hard, blue September sky. It was obviously another casualty of the air battle that had been raging over the English coast for the last month.

'Yes, Count,' he said.

'When I was a boy,' the Count said, smoothing down the long Roman Catholic soutane which he had recently taken to wearing, 'I knew an East Prussian Junker who thought he was a bird.'

Otto looked at his middle-aged partner, but said nothing. Since they had first met in that prison cell in Aachen in September 1939 he had got used to Graf von der Weide's strange ways.

The Count continued.

'Because of his little quirk, his servants – servants were very cheap in those days, though they were only Water-Poles – made him a nice nest in the oaks just to the front of the house. He would stay up there most of the day billing and cooing – oh, I forget to tell you, Otto, he imagined himself to

1

be a pigeon, just an ordinary one, not a racing pigeon. He was too portly for that, naturally.'

'Naturally!' Otto echoed, but sarcasm was always wasted on the silver-haired Count with the fleshy, handsome pale face. Otto flashed a glance to the line of wounded soldiers from the military hospital, waiting expectantly for the doors of the mobile brothel to open. They were a good crowd for a Wednesday, he told himself, and turned his attention to the Count again.

'Just before dinner, the servants would scatter a bit of seed at the base of the tree,' he continued, 'and he'd come down, pick at it a small while and then go inside to change for dinner. In those days in East Prussia, they always dressed, including military decorations on Sundays.'

Two amputees were limping up, pushing a basket-case to the head of the line, while the others grumbled. Further off, in the Bayeux Military Hospital's English section, the wounded prisoners jeered and gave raspberries.

'Typical Hun,' they called. 'Even needs a couple of other blokes to put him on the job!' Obviously understanding English, the basket-case pushed back his blanket to reveal that his pyjama flies were already open. He made an obscene gesture with his right hand, crying back, 'That's all you Tommies are good for – five against one. *Haw! Haw!*... Five against one!'

'Well, one day,' the Count continued, deigning as a man of the cloth, temporarily at least, not to notice the obscene ribaldry, 'the servants forgot to scatter the usual seed. The Junker didn't descend. That night it poured down – there's a lot of rain in that part of East Prussia, that's why the potatoes are so good.'

2

'Get on with it, Count,' Otto urged. 'It's nearly opening time.'

'Of course, my dear boy. We have to think of such mundane matters, I suppose. Well, the poor Junker got thoroughly soaked and caught pneumonia to which he unfortunately succumbed.' He stopped abruptly and stared down at the French priest's shovel hat which had been acquired by letting a local parson have a few minutes with the mobile brothel's latest reinforcement, a girl named Berlin Lola.

Otto Stahl's bright blue clever eyes took in that tragic look which the Count's face always bore when some crisis or other was in the offing.

'Now Count, don't let's have any moods. What's that little tale supposed to mean, now? Come on, cough it up. The customers are getting impatient. They'll be after poor old Leo's arse–' he indicated the dray horse in the shafts to the front of the converted Berlin furniture van which acted as accommodation for their four ladies of pleasure '– in half a minute.'

The Count hesitated.

Up at the barred window of the Tommies ward, one of the English had pulled down his pyjama trousers, stuck one of the midday salt herrings into his bottom and was hobbling around on his crutches, crying, 'Get me, fellers... I'm a mermaid!' It was obvious the English were envious of the men crowding up to the van below.

'Well, to be frank, Otto, I miss the eccentricity of the old days before we had to flee and take up this – er – *business*,' the Count said, measuring his tone for the benefit of his fine young friend.

3

LEO KESSLER

Otto looked at him incredulously. 'You mean the spy-school, with Admiral Canaris as Father Christmas, and the Jewish fascist Hirsch with his pigeon-shit, and Brass-Eggs, the warm brother who was always grabbing at your balls, and Gertie, the Commandant, dressed up as a female auxiliary all the time, and Maps... ' He gasped for breath. 'You don't *miss* them, do you?'

The Count nodded numbly.

'But *holy strawsack*,' Otto exploded. 'Why?'

'Because, my son, since we have won the war – or almost, save for those funny English over there – society has become very dull. Everyone is expected to conform.'

'Count,' Otto said, for he liked the middle-aged aristocrat who had saved him from the prison camp and perhaps even worse only months ago. 'We've got a nice little business going here. Four good girls who can service a whole company of infantry in one night and never a complaint from them, except perhaps that the stubble-hoppers might care to take their military boots off in bed now and again. We're in France, eat Chateaubriand steaks every night and swill them down with champagne, have a very decent frog mistress each–'

'I have decided to give Fifi up for the sake of the church, Otto,' the Count interrupted.

Otto ignored the interruption. 'Above all, Count, we're outside the Reich, free agents, with no *Gestapo* sniffing around all the time. What did you say when we took up this job – like Kings in France? Now, don't you–'

He broke off abruptly. Lola from Berlin, one of their girls, had just opened the door to the mobile brothel. She filled it completely, all three hundred pounds of her.

Leo, the dray horse, whinnied with the shock of the shifting weight and dug in its hooves grimly, twin jets of grey breath escaping from its distended nostrils.

A great cheer went up from the excited soldiers as Berlin Lola blew kisses from the doorway and cooed in a deep, gravelly baritone, 'Yoo hoo! Are my boys ready to party?' Her fluttering eyelashes nearly disappeared behind enormous rouged cheeks as she grinned a grin that showed off her gold-capped front teeth.

'I wish she wouldn't damn well do that,' Otto exclaimed, rising to his feet, as Leo, who acted as an animal brake when the van was fully operational, pawed the ground desperately to keep it balanced. 'She'll have poor old Leo kicking his hooves three metres in the air one of these days. Come on, Count, let's get down there and start the – collection fund.'

Together they hurried towards the van, while the soldiers crowded excitedly forward, five-mark coins in one hand, the issue rubber in the other.

'Take it easy, gentlemen!' Otto cried above the racket. 'Everybody will get his turn, don't worry. But just keep your money and your Parisian sheath at the ready. *Tempis fugit*, you know.'

'Not before me he doesn't,' the basket-case croaked, urging on the two comrades who were going to help him, a greedy look in his faded eyes. 'Let Tempis wait. I'm first, 'cos I'm not expected to last the day out.'

At the door the Count sighed and with an effort of will gave the man in the basket a dignified blessing. It was all just another day in the life of Occupied France.

***

France had been occupied for three months, and by this time the conquerors and the conquered had come to a *modus vivendi*. It was a very simple arrangement, motivated by money, food and sex.

The German conquerors paid and the French served: food and sex. But not to the ordinary *Wehrmacht* field-grey. At higher headquarters in Paris, it had been decided that the delights of *'la cuisine Francaise et l'amour Francais'* should be reserved for officers only. As General Stülpnagel, the Military Governor of Paris, had maintained when this vital question had been discussed by his staff – in secret, of course:

'Much too good for the rank-and-file, Mein Herren. Much too good! I mean, what will become of the *Wehrmacht* if the common-or-garden stubble-hopper gets to know about *Moet-et-Chandon* and *tripes a la Mode de Caen* and certain other little perversions which I will not mention in this place?' He leered at his officers knowingly through his monocle. 'No, gentlemen. We cannot allow our men to be perverted by such things. As from this moment, they are reserved for officers. After all, one has to be a gentleman to cope with such – er – piggeries.'

Thus Otto Stahl's mobile brothel filled a different niche. French ladies were out of bounds; therefore he supplied pure, unadulterated German instead, thanks to Leo's single horsepower, to his German soldier customers. He had taken to lecturing the ranks of field-grey, 'Now what do you fine upstanding young men want Frog ladies for, eh, when you have good homemade stuff on hand, checked, signed and sealed as fit for human consumption by high-ranking medical doctors in Berlin?'

Business boomed. Yet as Otto stood there that warm

September day outside the Bayeux Military Hospital – cricket bat in one hand in case of trouble (it had been abandoned by the Tommies at Dunkirk), the other full of hot five-mark pieces – he abruptly experienced some of the Count's dissatisfaction.

Chateaubriand steaks and his mistress Arlene's private performances, which she did exceedingly well, were all right in their place. But was running a mobile brothel the peak of his life achievements? It was an unnerving thought. Under his thoughtful gaze, the basket-case was wheeled out dead, but with a happy smile on his face.

Slowly but surely, Otto Stahl realised he was bored.

Otter-faced Admiral Keyes was standing ramrod straight, as befitted a well-decorated veteran of British military service. He was the head of Combined Operations, the Victoria Cross hero of Zeebrugge, and the deviser of bold but typically impractical schemes. One such scheme was set out in front of him on his desk. Papers, strategic drawings, and pencils littered its surface. A military issue waste basket was overflowing with crumpled papers by its side. He didn't need to look at the table to recount every detail of the plan – its next step was standing in front of him. Now that the terse pleasantries were over, he addressed his visitor with as stern an eye as he could muster.

'Now listen, A&D,' he snapped in that brisk naval fashion of his, staring down at the Laird of Abermockie and Dearth, the comical little commando with his drooping kilt and his shaggy mop of carrot-red hair, 'I'm going to ask you to do a tough job, although you've had hardly any training. But it's urgent, *damn* urgent!'

Outside in the other office, one of the Wrens was saying in an affected, middle-class voice, 'But, darling, our black stockings do contrast well with white underthings, don't you think? Imagine having to wear those khaki bloomers like the ATS, or even worse, grey like the WAFs. Unthinkable!'

The Admiral shook his head. 'Walls like paper, A&D. Boche espionage would have a field day here, *what?*'

The little Laird had once been an East End barrow-boy but, on the death of his uncle had inherited, to his astonishment, a castle, a couple of lochs, and half of the bleeding Scottish highlands. He was no fool, in spite of his ridiculous appearance and his private army, financed by the fortune that ten generations of canny Scots had built up. He was going to fight Herr Hitler, he was going to fight him in his own way. He ignored the question.

Instead he asked one of his own. 'What you got for me and the lads, Admiral?'

Keyes' otter-like features let slip a quick grin. Old A&D was a man after his own heart. 'Well, at the present moment we can tell the time from the clock on Calais' railway-station tower, but that's about all. We know virtually bugger-all about what's going over there on the other side of the Channel, and old Winnie's getting anxious. He wants to know.'

'Aye? And how do we come into it?'

'Very simple, A&D. We want bodies.'

'Alive or dead?'

'Alive, preferably,' Keyes answered, 'so that we can squeeze them. Then we can make a start at finding out what the Boche has planned in the way of an invasion of these here islands. We think that the Germans intend to invade across the shortest route – the Dunkirk, Calais area, heading for Kent. So we need some German prisoners from that area. You and a group of volunteers from your Commando are going to get those prisoners for us.'

The little Laird accepted the news calmly. After all it was the kind of assignment he had created his private army for in the first place. 'And how are we gonna get there, Admiral?'

Keyes, hard-bitten VC that he was, hesitated a moment. He knew how much some people were affected by the mere mention of the word; he had seen six-foot four marines go green when they were told the means of transportation for the job ahead.

'Sub!' he said. And then, quickly, 'Old Winnie thinks that a submarine is the safest means of getting across the Channel at the moment.'

'Submarine?' the Laird of Abernockie and Dearth croaked. 'And Old Winnie thinks that's safe. Now I *know* I should never have voted conservative.'

CHAPTER 2

The September sun blazed down. The sea sparkled a glassy afternoon grey. On the beach the shingle swayed back gently, creaking under the weight of the surf and Berlin Lola, who was prancing around in the water, her underskirt tucked into the elastic of her art silk pink knickers. The others watched her in lazy admiration, nibbling at their chicken legs and sipping lukewarm champagne, thinking that she looked every bit like a white hippo.

Over the white smudge which was England, the planes twisted and turned silently, their flight marked solely by white vapour trails. It was a perfect day for a Sunday picnic.

Otto took his eyes off a group of stiff-legged black and white birds hurrying back and forth along the beach like men on crutches. Leaning back, he yawned lazily.

'Could be a peacetime Sunday back on the Havel in Berlin, Count,' he announced.

The Count looked up from his breviary which he was reading, occasionally mouthing the Latin phrases, almost as if he were tasting the sonorous syllables.

'Oh… yes,' he commented with surprising acidity for him, 'just like a peacetime Sunday back home. Drinking champagne with four – er – *grandes horizontales* – and young men killing each other at two thousand metres in the sky over there. Very typical indeed.'

Next to him the consumptive whore Trina, who was slightly tipsy, lolled against the Count and breathed, 'Oh, Herr Graf, you do speak so lovely. I could just sit here all day and watch your mouth… drinking in your words.'

Otto took the half-bottle of champagne from her skinny fingers and said severely, 'Yeah, and that's all you're gonna be drinking in for the rest of this afternoon. Remember you've got the evening shift at Calais, and you know what this sea air does to the field-greys.'

The Count sighed again and Otto said, 'Now don't come crying stinking fish again, Count. That was what this picnic was about. To take your mind off things for a while.'

'But how can I, Otto?' The Count clapped his pudgy, well-manicured hand to his temple dramatically, his bright white eyes bulging out of his head like hard-boiled eggs. 'Tell me how!'

'Look, just tell me exactly what the problem is.'

'The absolute ennui of everything, Otto. Something must happen soon, or I shall go stark raving mad, I promise you.' As if in answer to his threat, it was at that moment that Berlin Lola fell into a rock pool and emerged laughing happily, pulling off her pink knickers to wring them out, and revealing a tremendous area of white flesh.

'See, Count,' Otto seized the opportunity offered him while the others laughed. 'That's something, ain't it? You don't see an arse like that every day of the week, even on Sundays, do you?'

'No,' the Count was forced to agree, 'young Lola is amply endowed.' Once again he gave one of his tragic sighs. 'But it is not the flesh, I seek, Otto.'

'Well, the only other thing on offer is this sodding war!' Otto said in exasperation. 'I'm going to hit the pit for half an hour.' He lay back in the sand and closed his eyes. Within a few minutes he was snoring softly. The Count stared down at his handsome face which had never seen defeat, only victory for a few moments. Then, being the kindly man he was, he took off his shovel hat and tilted the brim against the sleeping man's head to keep the sun off his face.

He sat there surrounded by the sleeping, snoring company, watching the silent planes looping and curling over England, as their pilots attempted to kill each other, and wished sadly that he was young again.

Lieutenant Brice-Jones, captain of His Majesty's Submarine Redwater, known throughout the Royal Navy as 'HMS Red Piss', thrust back his cap and commanded, 'Up periscope.'

The electric motor whirred and effortlessly the long tube steered for the surface, while the Laird watched the procedure, hollow-eyed and green-faced, quietly vomiting into the standard issue sick bag. The sea had been perfectly calm all the way from Portsmouth, but as the little Laird had moaned to his Second-in-Command, the Hon Freddie Rory-Brick (or 'Red Prick' as the men of the Laird's Command called him behind his back), 'Me, I'd get bloody sick going across Hackney Bridge, I would!'

The others waited in tense expectation, the sound of the submarine's electric motors dimmed almost to nothing.

Brice-Jones, his cap thrust back to front so that he looked like an early flier, swung the periscope round the clock, a puzzled look on his face until finally he said satisfied, 'Found it!'

'That's a relief,' the Laird said thickly.

The captain stepped back and ordered Down Periscope and then, 'Take her up,' before turning to the waiting commandos to say, 'You see I've never been abroad before, chaps. The war started the year we should have done our cruise at Dartmouth. But this looks like the place to me.' He stared around the heavily armed commandos, their faces blackened with boot polish so that they looked like a group of pre-war black minstrels.

'So this is the drill. We launch you now, dive, and rendezvous at twenty hundred hours.' He looked at his wristwatch. 'Shall we–'

'Circumcise our watches,' the Laird cut in angrily. 'Come off it, laddie, let's get this show on the road!'

Five minutes later the commandos started to scale the ladder into the conning tower. When it came to the Laird's turn, he held up his overlong kilt and began to ascend with difficulty, still giddy from seasickness.

At the base of the ladder, one of the ratings breathed in awe as the wind caught the Laird's kilt and blew it upwards, 'Airy, ain't it?'

'What did yer expect,' the Laird snarled, 'feathers?'

'It's a bit light up here, Colonel, I'm afraid,' the fresh-faced young captain apologized when the Laird clambered up beside him.

'A bit light!' the Laird exclaimed, squinting in the late afternoon sunshine that blazed on the perfectly calm sea, 'Christ, it's like bloody Wembley Stadium in the middle of a cup-final! Trust old otter-face Keyes to choose daylight for the mission. Now where's the outskirts of Calais?' he asked, knowing that they were a sitting duck out here if a German plane spotted them.

'I think over there – to the left somewhere,' the captain said, flushing a little. 'Perhaps I did make a slight miscalculation, after all.' He bit his bottom lip.

The Laird swept the coastline. It was empty of any kind of habitation. He stopped himself from exploding just in time. He knew now after a year of war that operations of this kind never turned out as planned and besides he was a kind man at heart; he didn't want to take it out on the embarrassed young naval officer.

Instead he said, 'All right, Captain, get those jolly tars mobile with the boats,' and turned to his men, muttering something about a lot of soft nellies with double-barrelled names who wore silk pyjamas.

Five minutes later the four canvas boats were on their way with the captain waving them goodbye from the conning tower and the Laird snorting, 'You'd think we was off on a day trip to Margate!'

Otto dreamed. Perhaps it was due to the wine and the hot sun, but it wasn't one of his usual dreams, full of compliant big-breasted women, who were only too eager to jump into bed with him. Instead it fringed on a nightmare, a mixture of fact and fantasy.

The location was Stralsund, where he had lived with his grandparents when his mother, 'the Witch', had gone on the trot in his native Berlin. She was earning her money as a lady of the night, or any time of day if it made her cash. Back then he had seen himself as a cocky, blond-haired Hitler Youth, complete with sam-browne and dagger.

Perhaps it was because it had been Hitler's Birthday, 20

April, but after the speeches and the parades and the eating and drinking, his troop of the Hitler Youth had gone on a private rampage in what was left of Stralsund's Jewish quarter.

They had found poor old Mayer, with his humpback and his carpet slippers, the front of his shabby waistcoat stuck full of pins and needles, and stained from years of dribbling his soup – the only Jew to venture out that fine April day. But then Mayer had always been regarded as slightly touched in the head; didn't he give credit to sailors?

Rolf, the leader of Otto's Hitler Youth troop, a burly sixteen year old who could flip dry peas off the end of his erection to a distance of twenty metres, much to the admiration of the younger members of the troop who were still trying to achieve the first stage of that particular trick, had been the one that had made the suggestion. 'Let's get the old Yid's pants down and have a look at a Jewish undercarriage, eh!'

The young boys had taken up the suggestion with delight. Surrounding the old tailor before he could shuffle off in his battered, ancient slippers. They had whipped out their ceremonial daggers, slashed through his braces, the buttons of his underpants, and left him standing there sobbing softly, exposed to their ribald comments.

Abruptly Otto had felt ashamed. He had never seen a grown man cry before and it hadn't seemed right that boys of eleven and twelve could do this sort of thing to an elderly man. Schulz, the fat-bellied local policeman had sauntered by. Otto hoped he would put an end to this torture, but the only comment he had made, at the sight of children taunting the half-naked adult, was: 'Now let that be a warning to you kids.

If yer don't behave yerself, the old uncle doctor'll have to cut a bit off your willies too!' And he had sauntered on his way, laughing at his own humour.

'Now then, you Yiddish garden-dwarf,' Rolf had chortled, complete master of the situation, 'now we're gonna see you bend over and receive a spanking from the Hitler Youth.' He waved his dagger, 'Or else, one dong is gonna to be a little shorter, if that's possible with that dingle-dangle you've got down th–'

He had never finished the threat, for Otto had slammed into him and started punching at Rolf's face with all his strength. The riot had started, with all Otto's one-time comrades piling onto him, slapping him across the face, crashing their boots viciously into his ribs until he had blacked out. The last thing he remembered was seeing the pale humble Jew's face with the tears streaming down it helplessly.

One day later he had run away from his grandparents' home, with its Hitler picture next to the crucifix, and fled back to Berlin to a life of petty crime, motivated by one thing: he would never serve the Hitler system, that vulgar, cruel, booted, brown-shirted terror which transformed boy scouts into sadists and perverts.

And now, years later, Otto mumbled and groaned in his sleep, as in his dreams he was confronted by thousands of old Mayers without their trousers. The beads of sweat gleamed on his handsome, sleeping face, while the Count stroked his head, muttering softly, 'Take it easy, Otto… take it easy, my boy… It's only a bad dream.'

They crept, slipping on the seaweed covered rocks, among the burnt-out, rusting fifteen-hundredweight trucks and smashed

Bren gun carriers, abandoned by the fleeing British Expeditionary Force three months before, some of them still bearing the proud boasts of 1939 on their sides.

'We're gonna hang out the washing on the Siegfried Line', 'Berlin or Bust!'

'I'm coming Adolf,' the Laird commented sourly. 'And I know where – not in Berlin!' He clambered over a stretch of rocks, and paused on the shingle beyond to stare up at the white chalk cliff that now confronted them. A gasping Freddie Rory-Brick halted next to him and stared upwards just in the same instant that a low-flying gull dropped a blob of white on his monocle. 'I say,' he said in disgust, 'doesn't make a fellow very welcome, does it?'

'Perhaps it was a Hun seagull,' the Laird said unfeelingly. 'All right, lads, I've had enough of this lark, tarting around all over the place. I think we're lost. Let's get to the top of that cliff and have a shufti where we're at, cos if I go farting around in the briny much longer, I'm gonna develop web feet.'

Hastily the three sergeants who were in charge of the grapnels broke out their equipment and, when they were ready, flashed a look at the little officer in his wet kilt.

'Fire!' he commanded.

The NCOs pressed their triggers. There were three soft belches followed by little puffs of white smoke. The three shining metal grapnels burst upwards, heading for the top of the cliff, followed by a hundred feet of snaking, quivering white rope.

Clang!

The first hook hit the top and bit metallically into the chalk. Then the second. The third hit the top and tumbled down again, clattering from rock to rock.

'I'm sorry, sir,' the NCO, whose grapnel hadn't found its mark, apologized, 'I don't think I've got my eye in this afternoon.'

'Yer, and I don't think you've got yer finger out either. But no matter, two will do. All right, laddies, up you go. I'm going up last. I'm not having any of you randy sods looking up my skirt again.'

The men laughed shortly and then they were scrambling up the ropes at a great rate, hardly seeming to touch the cliff with their boots as they scurried to the top like black-faced monkeys.

'Bash on, Jocks!' the Laird chortled. Carried away by a sudden enthusiasm, he scrambled after them, his wet kilt riding high up his skinny shanks unnoticed. A few minutes later he and Freddie were lying in the hot, cropped turf at the top of the cliff, panting hard, staring through their binoculars – at nothing but countryside.

'Where's Calais, sod it?' the Laird gasped.

'Well, it really ought to be here somewhere or other, sir,' his second-in-command said. 'I mean that naval chappie promised us it would be, didn't he?'

'Oh put the wood in the 'ole, Freddie,' the Laird snarled.

'Just trying to help, sir,' the former Scots Guards officer said in an offended voice. 'That's all.'

'Dammit, I didn't mean it, Freddie! Stop making me feel bad,' the Laird said, raising his glasses once more and sweeping the countryside to his right, covering each inch carefully until finally his binoculars ran along a low cliff leading down to a small secluded beach. He gasped abruptly and then with fingers that trembled slightly, hurriedly adjusted them. There was no mistaking it, that monstrous area of white female flesh which filled the gleaming circles of calibrated glass!

'What is it, sir?' Freddie asked urgently at his side, while the commandos tensed, fingers on their triggers at once. '*Jerries?*'

For a moment the little Laird did not answer, then he said in an awed voice, his eyes still glued to the glasses, 'No, Freddie. Not Jerries, but the biggest piece of female arse I've ever seen this side of Whipsnade Zoo!'

CHAPTER 3

Freddie whistled softly.

'It looks as if they've been having a picnic or something. Hardly patriotic, what?' He lowered his glasses from the sleeping figures and the huge pair of bloomers drying in the wind, looking like a small art silk bell-tent. 'I mean there is a war on, right?'

'Get off it, Freddie!' the Laird said. 'All of England has probably spent this weekend in the boozers, betting on the gee-gees and watching twenty-two strapping lads who claim they're C-3 unfit for active service, chasing after a soccer ball. You don't want to believe all that Churchill "we'll fight them on the beaches" stuff, old cock. If they invaded Arsenal Football Club, our lads might well fight, but not before.'

'I suppose you're right, sir,' Freddie said a little unhappily and sniffed. 'What now?'

'You speak the lingo, so don't stand there like one-of-each waiting for vinegar. Get over there and ask 'em.'

'Ask them what, sir?'

'Where the ruddy Jerries are, you silly sod.'

'But sir,' Freddie protested, flushing with embarrassment, 'we're commandos. We're supposed to be storming up the beach! You know, giving the Boche a taste of the cold steel.'

'Give them a taste of yer French – that'll be worse,' the Laird said drily.

'But one of the ladies is… er… without undergarments too, sir,' Freddie added unhappily.

'Get *on* with it,' the Laird hissed. 'Me and the Jocks'll cover ye. Now blow!'

Miserably, Major the Hon Freddie Rory-Brick 'blew'.

The Count looked up from his Latin prayer book, while all around him, Otto and the girls continued to snore open-mouthed, their faces red with the heat and the wine. A tall, skinny man in uniform was walking towards him across the sand, his face, for some reason, painted black.

The Count frowned and squinted into the late afternoon sun. Did the strange man belong to some sort of Goebbels' concert party, he wondered, sent from Berlin to entertain the bored field-greys of the coastal positions on a long Sunday? Then he dismissed the idea. Goebbels wouldn't have tolerated a German painting his face black. After all, Negroes were equated with apes in Berlin these days.

The tall stranger halted in front of the group lying in the sand, obviously trying to keep his gaze off Lola's sunburnt rump which protruded from the dunes like a small hill, flushing crimson in the first rays of the rising sun. He touched his hand to what looked like an old sock he was wearing on his head and said in hesitant French, '*Parlez-vous Francais, Monsieur?*'

'*Ah oui, biensur,*' the Count replied, lowering his book. '*Qu'est-ce que vous desirez, mon fils?*' he asked rapidly.

Freddie licked his lips a little desperately. '*Lentement,*' he said, waving his hand for the priest to slow down.

Probably some sort of Breton, the Count told himself. Their French wasn't too hot and, besides, the stranger did look a little bit like a Breton fisherman in his stocking cap, though for the life of him he couldn't work out why a fisherman needed to black his face. Was it a kind of primitive Breton custom, or perhaps some form of suntan oil? He smiled up winningly at the man.

Freddie smiled back, giving the Count the full impact of his horse teeth.

'*Bon,*' he said and then pulling out his whistle, blew three shrill blasts upon it.

Otto woke up with a start. The girls sat up, blinking rapidly. The Count, in character, pulled his robe about his knees. Suddenly there were similar black-faced figures racing across the sand everywhere.

'Where's the fire?' Otto spluttered, rubbing his eyes.

'Bimbos!' Berlin Lola cried with delight. 'Oh, how I love a real black bimbo!'

'To business, girls,' Trina announced, hastily beginning to remove her knickers. 'And watch it, girls, they're in a real hurry.'

Automatically the others began to do the same, while Freddie, slightly puzzled, beamed down at them and told himself they had to be speaking Flemish. There was a Flemish enclave on this part of the French coast.

The Laird came to a stop, his wet kilt flecked with sand, and gasped in his strong Scottish accent, 'Ask the frogs whether there are any Huns around here, Freddie.'

The Count couldn't understand. What was this other language? It was thick and guttural. Not French, not German, not Italian, not English. *Aha*, he thought, *they must be*

Flemish. There's a Flemish enclave on this part of the French coast.

Berlin Lola looked across at the Scot and whispered to Trina, 'Some sort of pervert – he's wearing a skirt.'

Freddie tried to take his eyes off the knickerless girls and said, '*Va-t-il les Allemands ice, m'sieu?*'

The Count frowned while he dissected this comically terrible pidgeon French. It seemed a particularly stupid question to him when they were all Germans here. Dutifully, however, he answered, wondering why this chap from the concert party insisted on speaking in French. '*Nous sommes Allemands, m'sieu!*'

Freddie's mouth dropped open stupidly.

'I say, sir,' he stuttered, 'they're Boche!'

The Laird's .38 revolver appeared like magic in his little fist.

'Hands up!' he barked.

Together Otto, the Count and the girls raised their hands, the menace understood, if not the words. Otto's mobile brothel had just become the first British captives in Europe since the debacle at Dunkirk.

At sea the Aldis lamp blinked on and off urgently. Beyond the horizon flickered a faint pink as the Luftwaffe bombers attacked Dover yet once again.

On the shore, the first boat pushed off, complete with wailing girls and their commando overseers. The Brits had taken all the girls save Berlin Lola. Back on the beach, she kept trying to flip up the Laird's kilt with a twig she had found, saying, 'I've got to know. I've just got to know whether they wear anything underneath.'

The Laird tried desperately to keep it down, crying, 'Fer Chrissake, missus, it's bloody drafty!'

'I expect,' Lola said excitedly, still poking at the Laird's kilt, 'he's knickerless just like me.'

'I've worked it out! They're Scottish,' the Count said over his shoulder as Freddie prodded him forward to the second boat. 'I have deduced this from his very aggressive-sounding speech. Scots are sort of savage tribe of the English. I think they paint themselves blue when they're beyond the supervision of the English King. But I do know they eat the insides of sheep and make music by blowing into a pig's bladder.'

'Ugh!' Berlin Lola said and stopped poking at the Laird's kilt, 'I don't think I'd like anyone who's bin eating sheep-guts.' She shuddered dramatically and all three hundred pounds of her trembled.

Sergeant MacGregor was impressed at the sight, but shoved the Count into boat number two and got in after him. Regretfully he took a last look at the big whore.

'Ach,' he said, 'yon wench has a nice pair of lungs on her. It's a rare shame to leave her behind, Laird. Besides them Jerries do have some good points – they kill the Frogs, for instance.' His eyes lit up hopefully for a second. 'Do you think we could take her back to Blighty with us, sir – for interrogation or something? Me and the Jocks would be glad to double up for her in the sub.'

'I know what you and the Jocks'd be glad to do,' the little Laird said severely from the beach. 'I don't think we'd stay afloat long with you lot poking holes in everything. Anyway we wouldn't be able to get her arse through the hatch in the top of the sub.'

And then the third boat was there and Otto was being led towards it, half-scared, half-excited, knowing somehow that a new phase of his life had just begun. For better or worse, his newly-found boredom was over for good.

'For you laddies,' the little Laird said as the sobbing girls began to fade away into the darkness and their craft came ever closer to the long low silhouette of TIMS Redwater, 'the war is over!'

'*Eh?*' Otto asked puzzled by the English. '*Was sagten Sier?*'

The little Laird wasn't disappointed that the prisoner had not understood his words. Instead he beamed at Freddie Rory-Brick and said happily. 'You know, Fred, I've been sodding well waiting to say that since September 1939 after I heard some feller say it in a pitcher at the old Rialto. Now I've finally done it.' Then his face changed colour and he said hurriedly in a thick voice, 'Fer Chrissake, Freddie, give me the vomit bag. I'm gonna puke!'

CHAPTER 4

The little Luftwaffe corporal with the nickel-framed, thick glasses, ripped open his flies and urinated somewhat short-sightedly into the wash basin containing three pairs of his socks.

'Like Persil,' he said, concentrating on the job in hand. 'Piss, I mean.' He finished and buttoned up the flies of his English battledress, complete with the blue patches of a POW sewn all over it. 'Gives your washing that final touch.'

'I'll give you the final touch, you dirty little bastard,' Otto said from his position on the wooden bunk, 'I've got to wash my face in that basin, you know!'

'Nothing wrong with piss,' the corporal said easily, obviously not bothered by his new cell mate's threat. 'Makes your eyes sparkle.'

Otto sighed and gave up, slipping back into a thoughtful silence once more while across the Channel the great German coastal batteries thundered, giving Dover the benefit of the usual evening hatred.

He had been in England three days now. They had landed at Portsmouth where the funny little Englishman in the skirt had patted him kindly on the arm and, with the aid of the Count as interpreter, had comforted him with, 'Don't take it to heart, son. Bit o' bad luck, that's all, especially having to leave those good-looking bints behind as well. But cheer up, you're seeing the world now.' And he had swaggered off at the head of his black-faced ruffians. Two years later he would sail from that same port to meet his violent death at Dieppe, in that famously disastrous raid. But Otto would never learn of that.

Thereafter he and the Count had been taken in a heavily escorted convoy through the Southern English countryside, beautiful and green in the late September sunshine, with the Count giving an excited running commentary, until they had reached the grim case of an embattled Dover, where they had been separated into their own isolation cells.

There Otto had remained in solitary confinement for forty-eight hours, his only contact with the outside world an elderly soldier who thrust plates of cold food at him three times a day and a chipped mug of scalding hot tea, each time grunting only one word: 'Grub!'

It was to be the first word of English he would learn.

Then suddenly this very morning, the elderly soldier, who he saw now wore battered carpet slippers, had beckoned him to another cell, in which he had found the little short-sighted corporal. The man's habits weren't exactly social, but at least he was someone to talk to. Maybe this chap had information he could piece together into some sort of incredibly daring and intelligent plan. That would be sure to impress the Count von der Weide. *Hell*, thought Otto, *I bet he's loving every minute of his new-found career as Prisoner Of War*.

The ancient walls shuddered for one last time as the evening hate ended, the plaster drifting down from the roof like sad grey flakes of snow. Otto, his ears ringing in the sudden silence, asked, 'Now that's over, how did you get here, mate?'

The little corporal looked up from his socks. 'Special invitation of King George.' His accompanying wink was magnified in the thick lens. 'Asked me over to Buckingham Palace to have a cup of tea and a cream cake with him and his missus. God shave the King!' He stood to attention and raised his sock-clad hand to his forehead in mock salute.

Otto grinned. *This little corporal's a bit of a card*, he thought. 'Come off it! How did you really get here?'

The corporal's grin disappeared. 'The usual Luftwaffe balls up,' he said. 'My squadron, the Eleventh Bomber stationed at Evreux, was scheduled for a raid on the East End of London. That's where the docks are, I think. Anyway, I'm sitting in the wet canteen, enjoying a quiet beer with my pals, and the squadron sergeant-major comes charging in saying, "Where's Schmidt?" – that's me – "We need a relief radio operator. Heinz has gone and got himself the pox from some frog girl!"'

The corporal's face showed just what a shock that must have been for him. 'I said, "What me, Sergeant-Major? But I've not been certified fit for flight duties. Besides I've got glasses as well."' The corporal paused for a dramatic sniff. 'Didn't worry the big bastard one bit. He said, cheeky as well, "I hereby, certify you fit for flight duties – and stick those glasses in yer pocket. I don't want the pilot to see you wearing them."

'I sez, "But I'm blind as a bat without them."

'"Don't worry," he sez, "I'll lead you over to the aircraft."'

In the prison cell, the corporal shook his head in mock

wonder. 'You wouldn't think it possible, would you, eh? But that's the way Fat Hermann –' Otto knew that was Reich Marshall Goering, the head of the Luftwaffe '– is running the war. Somebody ought to tell the *Führer* about him.'

'And what happened then?'

'What do you think, mate?' the corporal answered sourly. 'Oberleutnant Schmitz, our arsehole of a pilot, couldn't find London! Imagine that, couldn't find London, a city with ten million inhabitants and covering hundreds of square kilometres, and it was bright as day – full moon!'

Otto laughed out loud, but quickly managed to add a sympathetic edge to the sound. 'And then?'

'We must have cruised up and down the length of the Thames looking for the damn place for hours. Then the engines started to spark and splutter and Schmitz sings out, "We're running out of juice. Better get prepared to bail out, fellers." *Bail out!* I nearly shat in my hat!'

The little corporal's face grew pale in the light of the cell's electric lamp, bright now in the waning light. 'Hell, I get dizzy standing on a step-ladder and I told him so over the intercom. But all the silly shit could say was, "Well it's either that or a watery grave, Corporal, because we'll be over the big drink in thirty seconds or so!" So what could I do?'

'You jumped?'

'Yeah, I jumped. And do you know what happened then?'

The corporal looked expectantly at Otto through his glasses. After a moment, Otto became a little uncomfortable. 'No,' he admitted.

'The bloody engines picked up and here I am sailing down towards England and the Dornier's off at full throttle heading for the officers' mess and free frog champus. The Bavarian barnshitter had just forgotten to switch over to the reserve gas tanks. "*Wir fahren gegen England*," my arse! If all our brave fly-boys are like Oberleutnant Schmitz, we'll be invading England in the year 2000,' he said with a sneer.

For a few moments Otto absorbed the indignant little corporal's story, then he said, 'What kind of place is this, anyway?'

'Arsehole of the world, if you ask me. It's an interrogation centre. Didn't they tell you about these places in your unit?' he looked at Otto curiously.

'What unit?'

'Come off it, mate, your battalion. Anyway, they try to pump you here, squeeze out some information, and they keep you here till you sing. Their trick is that Dover – we're under some sort of fallen-down castle – is being bombarded by our own gunners off Calais. You see the irony of it, apart from the danger, your own people blow you to eternity.'

'But what do they want to know?' Otto asked. 'How to run a travelling knocking shop?'

'Your unit, the number of men in it, your weapons and the like. I've told them the lot, especially about that Bavarian banana-sucker Schmitz. Serves him right if they put a Tommy torpedo right up his elegant arse one of these days. *Bail out!*' he sniffed again, indignantly. 'That's why I'm washing me socks. I'm off to a POW camp tomorrow morning.'

Otto's handsome face wrinkled into a frown and there was a worried look in his deep blue eyes. 'Unit, number of men, weapons?' he echoed unhappily. 'The only weapons we ever had were between the legs of –'

'What?' the little corporal exclaimed in astonishment.

31

'Yes, exactly,' Otto said miserably. 'They'll never believe my story. I'll be here for all eternity.'

Corporal Rubinstein, still clad in his POW uniform, swung the seated officer a tremendous salute and nearly knocked himself over.

'Permission to speak, sir?' he barked, as if he were on the parade ground.

'Yes, yes, of course,' the Intelligence Corps captain said, holding his right hand to his ear with a pained look on his face. 'I asked you a question didn't I? But please don't shout so much, Corporal. After all, we're not at the Guards Depot at Pirbright, you know.'

'Sorry, sir!' the little corporal barked.

'Oh come off it, Rubinstein, don't play bloody Grenadier Guardsmen with me. Permission to speak indeed!' Captain Wanke-Smythe smiled. The 'Wanke' had been passed down by his mother's father, much to the mirth of the fellows at Oxford. They'd called him Smith the Wanker. 'Well, Rubinstein, what did you find out about him?'

'Not much, sir,' Rubinstein replied, his professional pride hurt.

'Well, have you found out something, man?'

'I did, sir. But I think it's a come-on.'

'What do you mean?'

'You'll hardly believe this, sir.'

'Try me,' Wanke-Smythe said cynically. 'Since I joined the Intelligence Corps I have heard tellings that even a Jehovah Witness wouldn't believe.'

'Well, sir, he maintains that he was running a mobile brothel for the troops when our commandos grabbed him.'

'A *what?*'

'A knocking shop on wheels, sir. A travelling tart house. A perambulating prostitute parlour. A naked –'

'Dammit, man, I get the idea!' Wanke-Smythe's dark eyes lit up. 'You know, Rubbie, old boy, I think we're on to something here. Yes, I do believe we've hit the jolly old jackpot.'

'How do you mean, sir?' Rubinstein said, infected by his officer's sudden enthusiasm.

'Last night I interrogated the other one who dresses up as a priest, and do you know what I found out?'

'No, sir,' Rubinstein breathed leaning forward in eager anticipation.

'He once worked for Admiral Canaris.'

'What, the mastermind of the *Abwehr*?'

Wanke-Smythe tapped the end of his long beaked nose significantly. 'And my dear old Rubbie, he might well be working for Canaris still.'

'But what he's doing dressed as a priest and helping run a mobile brothel – if the other chap's statement is true?' Rubinstein protested. 'Sounds more like he needs his marbles checking to me, sir.'

'Don't be too hasty in your judgements, Rubbie,' the captain said calmly. 'Cunning buggers these Boche, you should know. It's probably all part of a plot, a very deep plot, believe you me.' He sucked his yellow teeth and frowned hard so that the little corporal couldn't help thinking he looked a little like Basil Rathbone doing his Sherlock Holmes act. 'Try the blond Hun you're inside with once again,' he declared finally.

'I told him I was being moved to a POW camp

tomorrow, sir.'

'Well, have a go at him tonight, while I work on the Father.'

Rubbie clasped his hands together, as if in prayer, and rolled his dark eyes piously towards the ceiling. 'Let us pray, brethren,' he intoned.

Smith the Wanker laughed. 'Be off with you, you irreverent Jewish rogue!'

'I don't know about your officers, pal,' the little corporal said as they sat facing each other in their wooden bunks, eating the evening meal of corned-beef sandwiches and cocoa. 'But you wouldn't believe the things that happened at Evreux when the gentlemen officers started hitting the sauce in the mess. Like kids they were.'

Otto sipped his sugarless cocoa morosely and said nothing. His cellmate had already packed his meagre kit in a brown paper parcel ready for his departure tomorrow; then he would be alone in the place again.

'Our CO, for instance. He'd get as high as a howitzer every Saturday night – regular. By midnight he'd be stripping off his uniform, save his ceremonial sword and jackboots, staggering all over the field with his dingle-dangle covered by his cap, shouting that it was on account of personal modesty and he didn't want to give the female auxiliaries stationed at Evreux a shock. They'd get screaming heebie-jeebies when they saw the size of it, he said.' He shook his dark head in mock disgust.

Still Otto said nothing, his unhappiness forgotten a little now as he concentrated on where he had heard a similar intonation to that of the corporal before. Why, he didn't exactly know. Outside the sirens started to give off their thin, frightening wail, indicating that soon Dover was in for another Stuka dive-bombing attack.

'Then there was Phyllis the Padre.'

'Phyllis is a funny name for a padre,' Otto said, intrigued, breaking his silence for the first time.

The little corporal winked and said, 'He was that kind of padre.'

'Oh,' Otto said and finished the last of his cocoa before the vibrations of detonating bombs upset the liquid.

'One time he came back from the mess full of sauce, staggered into my billet, crying his head off and howling, "mea culpa". I think it's some kind of Latin war cry. Then he tried to get in my bunk with me, telling me he was going to explain all about the Immaculate Conception and it would be cosier under the blankets. And when I wouldn't wear it, he went down on his knees, still crying and asking me to flog him "for the good of my soul!" I told him he could sod his soul, and that it was for the good of my arse. Next day he got me seven days jankers from the CO for disobeying a direct order! Ever afterwards when I met him, he'd sniff, "God and I will have nothing more to do with you, you ungrateful wretch." Just like that, as if he had a god-damn direct line to Heaven!'

Otto laughed shortly. Now outside the British 3.7 anti-aircraft guns were beginning to thunder, but even they could not drown the roar of engines. 'Here they come with their square eggs,' he said.

The danger did not seem to worry the little corporal. 'Oh, don't worry about those Stuka shits,' he said, carelessly. 'They couldn't hit a turd in a piss-pot.'

Otto shrugged. 'If you say so–' the rest of his words were drowned by the sirens and howling air-brakes of a diving Stuka, hurtling out of the sky at 400 kilometres an hour. Otto could visualize the gull-winged dive-bomber flailing out of the night at an almost ninety-degree angle, as if the pilot would never be able to stop it plunging straight into the ground.

The first stick of bombs hit Dover. A series of thick, obscene crumps. The walls of their cell trembled. Plaster came raining down. A second stick sounded much closer. The third blew them both from their bunks onto the stone floor, the cell suddenly flooded with the hot acrid stink of burnt cordite. The lights flickered and went out abruptly.

'Great buckets of fire!' the little corporal gasped. 'Fat Hermann's boys might just go and croak us after all!'

And then Otto had it! On the floor, he clicked his fingers together with the excitement of his discovery, while outside the world rocked and trembled – like a ship at sea struck by a sudden hurricane – under the impact of the bombs, and hot blast came rushing into their cell to strike them across their faces like a blow from a damp, flabby fist.

'Hey, you're from the coast – the Baltic coast!' he roared above the howl of the Stuka's sirens and the thump-thump-thump of the flak.

'What?' his cellmate asked, getting back to his feet. Otto followed his lead.

'From the Baltic Coast?' Otto yelled, his mouth close to the other man's ear in the flickering pink and darkness.

'Yes... Yes! But what–'

'Stralsund?' Otto hazarded a wild guess.

'Yes. Heaven, arse and cloudburst, yes, Stralsund! And

if you're so bloody well eager to know, Georg Fockstrasse, to be exact!' He gasped. 'What a time for old home-week!'

Otto knew now where he had heard accents like that before. From the Jews who lived all around old Mayer, the tailor, who was foolish enough to give credit to sailors. 'You're a Jew, aren't you?' he bellowed above the blast and thunder of another stick of bombs.

'A what?'

'You're a god-damn Hebrew Jew!' Otto roared.

In a sudden burst of purple flame, Otto caught a glimpse of the little corporal's face, the usual good-humoured look had vanished, to be replaced by one of almost wolfish determination, the eyes bulging, the lips bared to reveal yellowish teeth. 'Don't try anything,' he hissed over the patter of falling plaster. 'You're bigger and more powerful than me, you Nazi bastard! But I'll make you pay, I'll make—'

As the cell swayed and heaved, the little corporal faced him, fists doubled, ready for action.

Very gently, Otto reached out a hand and patted him on the shoulder, saying as quietly as he could yet still make himself heard, 'Don't worry, Corp, I'm not going to hurt you. All I want is for you to do me a favour.'

'A favour?' the other man echoed, as the lights flickered back on and the roar of the Stuka engines began to die away, only to be replaced by the first thin wail of the all-clear.

'Yes. Get me out of here,' Otto said simply, as the other man dusted down his knees and sat back on his bunk. 'I know nothing of military value. Honest, I *am* what I say I am – the owner of a mobile brothel.'

'You want out of here – to where?' asked the corporal.

'To a camp where I can be with my own people.'

'Germans?' Rubinstein spat out the word, as if it were dirty.

Otto nodded humbly and said a little sadly. 'Yes, Germans. They are the only people I've got, friend.'

It might have been that Otto's wish to be put with his fellow countrymen might not have been fulfilled so promptly, but for a priority telephone call that Captain Wanke-Smythe received later that night.

He was lying in his bunk in a corner of his office, working as usual through a bottle of NAAFI whisky in order to forget Dover, the Interrogation Centre, and the bombardment. He realised he hadn't had a woman since the girl he'd picked up in Piccadilly Circus on his last forty-eight hours. He smiled, remembering that the blackout had been so effective he hadn't been able to see her face. They had done it up against Eros, which had seemed suitably symbolic. It was into this epic reverie that the rattle of the phone injected itself wholeheartedly.

For a moment or two he stared at it drunkenly, the words of the current hit – 'Dear little henny, when, when will you lay me an egg for my tea' dying on his lips.

Then he fumbled for it, upsetting the pile of new leaflets from the Ministry of Information entitled, 'What To Do If Invasion Should Come!'

'Run like hell, I should think,' he snarled drunkenly and picked up the receiver. 'Are they landing?' he said thickly.

'Stand by, sir, for a top-priority messnge, sir,' a metallically distorted prissy female voice said. 'You are Captain Wanke-Smythe, aren't you sir?'

'No, Smith the Wanker,' he snapped icily. 'Of course, I'm him... er,' vaguely he remembered that he had been educated at Oxford, 'I mean he. Who wants me?'

'One moment, sir, please,' the prim, professional telephonist said.

There was a series of clicks, while he stared with blurred eyes at the leaflet, trying to make sense of a paragraph that commenced,

> *Now how do you know that this lone nun*
> *is an enemy parachutist? First you must*
> *remove the top part of the supposed nun's*
> *habit. You will see immediately by the*
> *nature of the suspect's anatomy if you*
> *have made an unfortunate error.*
> *However, if you have been correct in your*
> *assumptions, you will find the typical red*
> *marks made by a parachute harness –*

'Captain Wanke-Smythe?' The voice metaphorically tapped him on his shoulder. It was upper-class, heavy with Eton, the Brigade of Guards, inherited money – and power. It was the voice of authority.

It sobered the Intelligence Corps captain up immediately. Symbolically, he swung the unknown speaker a tremendous salute which left his fingers quivering just below his hairline in the approved drill-sergeant's fashion.

'Sir!' he barked.

'Come here,' the voice said. 'I've read your report. Drop everything. Bring Graf von der Weide to my office in Broadway immediately. Lose the other chap. Thank you.

Good-night, Captain.'

Abruptly the phone went dead, leaving an astounded Captain Wanke-Smythe staring at it, as if a little green man had just emerged from the thing and blown him a raspberry. He had just spoken to C!

CHAPTER 5

By the autumn of 1940, York, that northern grey Gothic cathedral town, had almost forgotten the war. After all, the Siege of York by the Roundheads in 1644, had been more slightly momentous than this so-called World War.

But back in September 1939 the barracks had filled up with reservists and there had been electric excitement in the air. That time, just one year ago, now seemed long gone.

A little panic had broken out when rationing had been introduced and for a couple of days the better-off bought all they could lay their hands on. Beaverbrook's scrap-metal drive had caused another ripple of excitement, and the trophy cannon dating back to the Crimean War, plus most of the city's railings had disappeared over night (even today there are Yorkists who hiss 'traitors' when they pass one of the innumerable Victorian houses of the city where the railings are still intact).

What followed was boredom. Once or twice the sirens sounded, and excited little boys who knew that if the 'all-clear' did not sound by midnight they would be free from having to go to school the following morning, prayed to God to let the 'Jerries' come. Obstinately, the 'Jerries' refused to come, and come the morning, the boys went to their schools.

Thus it was that while Britain battled for its supposed

existence in the south, York had settled back into being the northern provincial backwater that it had been for the last three hundred years, ever since the Cavaliers had been sent packing by the Roundheads, and the cause of Charles I had ended on the executioner's block.

It was to this remote northern city that Otto came, in the company of a cross-eyed army cook, who had gone fishing off the Normandy coast and, to his great surprise, found himself in Kent with not even a mackerel to show for his pains; an arrogant, wooden-headed air-gunner, shot down over London; a mild-mannered, bespectacled 'Bible Student' who had been conscripted into the *Wehrmacht* against his will and had rowed fervently across the Channel to escape; and fifty happy bronzed Italians who had surrendered cheerfully in the Western Desert the month before.

The train journey passed in a blur for Otto. His mind was confused. Where was the Count? He could have been enjoying himself if the Count was here – a curious kind of enjoyment that mostly involved devilishly dangerous plans, yes. But enjoyment all the same.

Otto hadn't seen his compatriot since the day of their imprisonment. Maybe his upper-class roots entitled him to a better class of incarceration. Oh well, for the moment, he was on his own. And there was only one thing for it: if the Count wasn't providing the adventure, then Otto would have to get off his arse and do it himself. He'd have to escape!

After the brain inside that tousled mop of blond hair had come to this conclusion, Otto had sat back and watched the landscape trickle past. His new companions certainly were a strange bunch: cook, student, air-gunner, and fifty nattering Italians. He'd take his time and see how this played out.

***

The lot of them arrived on a sunny morning in October 1940.

'This is York Station,' the female announcer whispered furtively through the loudspeakers, as if she suspected that German agents lurked everywhere. The prison train came to a shuddering halt. Its engine gave out a great cloud of steam that shot high to the roof of the huge Victorian station.

The elderly volunteer with the blue rinse in charge of the 'Forces Canteen' readied herself for the onslaught of customers. 'It's no use asking for cups,' she yelled towards the train, "cos I know you common soldiers, you just break them! There's only jam jars.'

At the barrier the two hawk-faced redcaps, whose eyes were hidden beneath their peaked hats, straightened up and began looking officious. The fat, elderly railway policeman, proud of his new revolver, touched his holster significantly like Tom Mix and stared with narrowed eyes at the prisoners-of-war now emerging from the train. It was the hard look of a born killer.

'All right, all right, now,' the middle-aged staff-sergeant in charge of the transport cried above the clatter of steel wheels and the rush of escaping steam, 'sort yerselves out! Come on, now, let's be having you there!'

They were let out into the big square in front of the station, stared at by curious school children waiting for their buses. Some youngsters ate stale sandwiches from their cardboard gas-mask containers and occasionally called out at the beaming Italians, 'Knock knock. Who's there? *Abyssinia*. Ah be seeing yer after the war. Ha, ha!'

For a few moments there was a little scuffle between the air-gunner and the Italians as to who should lead the march to the POW camp. The air-gunner insisted the four Germans should; the Italians replied that they were in the majority, therefore they should lead. In the end the middle-aged staff sergeant decided the Italians would.

'You wops are all the same size,' he bellowed above the laughter and jeers of the schoolkids, 'and you've all got the same hair colour. You Jerries come in all shapes and sizes. The Eyeties go first. Got to make a decent orderly impression on the natives, you know. All right, let's be off and bags of swank, you Eyeties. Show the locals what you're made of!'

They set off at a slow shuffle, surrounded by soldiers armed with fixed bayonets, led by the now very self-important staff sergeant, swinging his arms as if he were leading a pre-war Empire Day parade, crying loudly, 'One, two, three, four! Left... right! Swing them arms now!'

The wooden-faced air-gunner looked at the chattering crowd of Italians who strolled through the shabby streets of the ancient city as if they were on one of those evening walkabouts so common in their native land.

'What a shower of shit, the spaghetti-bending buggers! Comrades, we've got to show these buck-teethed Tommies what we Germans are made of.'

The column came to a ragged halt in front of a traffic light, which was at red, while the NCO in charge clapped his swagger stick impatiently against his leg.

'Now then, comrades,' the air-gunner said urgently, 'we're gonna give them a song, a real German marching-song.'

'Oh, my aching back!' Otto groaned.

But there was no stopping the air-gunner now. '*Einsy zweiy drei – ein Lied,*' he commanded.

In the very instant that the lights changed to green and the shabby column shuffled off once more, he burst into the *Horst Wessel Lied*, '*Die Fahne hoch, die Reiheti fest geschlossen...*'

Reluctantly the other three Germans joined in. The British NCO beamed. 'That's the stuff to give the troops,' he said enthusiastically. 'Nice bit of singing by the Army always impresses the civvies. All right you Eyeties, show a bit of regimental spirit! Hum, if you don't know the words. There'll be an extra ration of five Woodbines for the lot of you, if you do!'

The bribe worked. The Italian prisoners started to hum the marching song, aided by the whistling Tommies, who were infected by its lively manner. Thus it was that Otto Stahl arrived at his place of imprisonment, singing the *Horst Wessel Lied*, the aggressive anthem of the National Socialist Party, with his guards whistling lustily at his side. Somehow it seemed appropriate to Otto, who had long since decided that the world of men was absolutely crazy.

Captain Harry Hawkins, Camp Commandant, beamed with pleasure at the singing and whistling that floated up to his office high in the stands of what had once been York Race Course. His new prisoners seemed a happy bunch at least, and he told himself, 'a happy prisoner meant a happy camp commandant'. It was then that the Camp's senior NCO, Staff-Sergeant Dicks came in through the door, his face flushed with excitement, and flung Hawkins a tremendous salute, his boots smashing down on the stone floor.

'That's a bunch of scoundrels and a half, Dicksey,' Hawkins said. 'Good news?'

Dicks, who had just 'signed' for the newly arrived prisoners, said excitedly, 'You bet, sir. Fifty-four.'

Captain Hawkins's leathery, scraggy bird-of-prey face lit up. 'Christ, Dicksey,' he exclaimed, 'we're in the money at last. Our ship's come home. Now they can't wind up the camp, the shite-hawks. All Eyeties?'

'No, sir. Four squareheads among them.'

'Oh, we'll soon settle the hash of any loose wallahs among them.' Hurriedly he got to his feet and crossed to the big chart on the wall, while Dicks waited with bated breath.

He erased the previous figure at the bottom of the chart which was entitled 'Enemy POW Strength –Oct, 1940' and did a quick mental calculation. Then, with a hand that trembled slightly, he crayoned in the new total. He stood back to let Dicks see the figure. This lovely number meant they were now safe in this cushy billet.

'104, mixed Eyeties and Squareheads!' Dicks breathed. 'Now we guards are at last outnumbered by the prisoners.'

'Jolly good!' Hawkins said enthusiastically. 'There'll be no going back to square-bashing for you now, Dicksey. We're in the business. Northern Command can't close us up now. 104 POWs! It's pukka, Dicksey, very bloody pukka indeed.'

Dicks wiped the sweat off his fat, well-fed face. Like his commander Hawkins, he had got his 'feet under the table' with a widow-woman in York and was being well looked after in both senses of the word. He said, 'I must admit, sir, I'd already got my kitbag packed and my webbing blanched.'

Hawkins walked across to the filing cabinet and opened the door marked 'Light Entertainment' to produce a bottle of whisky. 'I know the sun hasn't gone down yet, Dicksey. But I think this calls for a bit of a celebration. What about a wee dram? The glasses are over in the corner.'

Captain Harry Hawkins had been a quarter-master sergeant with an infantry battalion for twenty years in India by the time 1939 graced the pages of his daily diary. In those two decades he had gone virtually native. He had enjoyed the native women, taken to eating pilau in rancid ghee, and had adopted Indian sanitary habits that *didn't just* include hawking and spitting after virtually every second sentence and cleaning his nostrils in public. Those in the know were very canny about giving Quarter-Master Sergeant Hawkins a handshake and the occasional outbreaks of dysentery were always traced back to him by the medics.

It had come as an unpleasant surprise when he was ordered to France with his Battalion. Indeed it was a surprise for the whole command. They had arrived on the Western Front in a raging snowstorm, dressed in starched shorts and solar topees, with officers who still carried swords. Hawkins hadn't liked the food, the women, the cold, and above all, the fighting.

In June 1940, he had brought out what was left of B Company at Dunkirk and had been awarded the MBE (Military Division), an immediate commission for bravery in the field ('I nicked some abandoned frog trucks before a bloke in the next battalion did', he confessed later to drinking buddies). Thereupon he had promptly got himself downgraded temporarily, while he looked around for a safe billet.

The York POW Camp had been right up his street. He knew immediately that if he played his cards right, it would provide him with 'the cushy number' he needed until he could go back to India and the world he understood and loved: char in the charpoy, and such. There, he would serve out the next thirty years until he got his pension.

His one problem in this cunning little plan? Not enough prisoners to warrant keeping the York Camp open. Now that he had those prisoners, his only worry was keeping the bastards!

CHAPTER 6

'It was once an English racecourse,' Pastor Mueller, the camp's senior German, explained. 'They've tried their best to make it into a prison camp, but they haven't done a good job.' Pastor Mueller was dressed in a shabby, blue suit. The only indication that he was a man of the cloth was a black pullover with white, tie-less collar protruding from it. He pointed to the straddled wooden-legged watch-towers some ten metres high, each housing sentries armed with Bren guns, complete with searchlights on the parapets used to illuminate the huts set below inside the triple barbed-wired fences. 'Look closely. Their chaps are rather old and a little careless.'

'Of course,' the wooden air-gunner sneered, as the newcomers moved on in their guided tour of their new home. 'Typical Tommy. Completely inefficient. Didn't even note the scar on my backside when I had my particulars taken.'

'Perhaps they were too polite,' Pastor Mueller suggested mildly.

'Lazy, that's what it was,' the air-gunner snapped. 'All a bunch of perverts anyway. Like to be beaten by canes, they do, and that's just what they deserve.'

'You might have been lucky, then,' Otto suggested, 'that they didn't want to look at your arse – excuse me, Pastor, please!' he added hastily to the camp's senior German.

Pastor Muelle was a rotund, middle-aged man with a mouthful of gold teeth and a twinkle in his faded blue eyes. He waved a pudgy hand and said, 'Not to worry, my boy. I was in charge of the Lutheran Mission to German Seamen in Hull for eighteen years. I can assure you I have heard worse things in my time, much worse.'

The air-gunner glared at Otto.

They wandered on through the camp, with Otto noting that, in spite of the careless guards, the barbed-wire fence was new and taut. Some effort would be needed to get across it, especially as there were little sign points running its whole length stating that any prisoners moving within one metre of it would run the risk of being shot. He wondered, for a moment or two, if there might be any chance of getting under it, then dismissed the thought.

'You must realise, comrades,' Pastor Mueller was saying, 'that we're slightly peculiar in this place, naturally.'

The air-gunner took his eyes off an Italian who wore an ankle-length evening gown made of black-out material and was painting his lips delicately with the aid of a mirror held up adoringly by a burly companion, and whispered hoarsely, 'That I can see.'

'Sometimes I wish I had not taken over this task.' Mueller smiled at the four new Germans a little sadly. 'If I had not been a Catholic priest, I would have automatically been classified as an officer and gone elsewhere. But the Tommies must have some sort of prejudice against us. So I am classified as an NCO and land here.' He sighed. 'It is all very strange.'

'The Whore of Rome,' the air-gunner said hotly.

The pastor sniffed, and pointed to a little hut all by

itself a little way from the other buildings, and closest to the wires. 'The Hole,' he explained. 'That's where they send the bad boys.'

'Bad boys?' Otto queried.

'Yes, any of our people who break the commandant's rules. One of the Italians is in there now for having eaten the captain's cat. The skin didn't flush down the lavatory properly, and was traced back to him. Ten days for "unnatural consumption of domestic animals" – that's what the commandant called it. The Italians say cats are a great delicacy in their own country. Taste like rabbit.' He shrugged. 'Interesting place the Hole. Very well located.' He glanced at Otto, a searching look in his eyes, as if he expected something of him. 'Very well located indeed.'

They walked on slowly, while the pastor explained the hobbies and recreations the camp offered, poor as they were, concluding with the information, 'Of course we have our weekly tea dancing punctually at four o'clock on Saturday afternoon. It breaks up the long weekend. A small extra ration of cornflour to be used as face powder and charcoal for doing the eyebrows are available for those so inclined.

'We prefer our people not to dance with the Italians if possible, and naturally too intimate a contact during tangoes and fox-trots is *verboten*.' He winked at Otto, who echoed, 'Naturally.'

Otto's eyes had been darting over every aspect of the camp during Muelle's talk, but now he took in the pastor properly for the first time. Somehow or other he thought there was more to the senior German than met the eye.

Blond-haired, young Otto Stahl settled into the simple but safe routine of prison camp life. Food was the first consideration, as always in such places. As Pastor Mueller would often maintain, quoting Brecht, '*erst kommt das Fressen, dann kommt die Moral.*'

In the main it consisted of corned beef, which the inmates called 'monkey-flesh'; kohl-rabi, known as 'cold-rabbi' or 'chilled Yid'; and the soft English white bread so abhorrent to the German taste. It soon became obvious that the air-gunner was a complainer: 'Christ, how can a man crap with that white stuff inside yer? It doesn't give a man's guts anything to grab onto. What a people, the Tommies, they chill their baths, boil all their bloody grub, including the bread, and they warm their beer! No wonder they're a bunch of warm-brothers, with nasty complexions and rotting teeth.'

Tackling the English language was the second consideration. Whatever his next move was going to be, an understanding of the enemy's native tongue would help matters considerably.

The time would pass with grub, a lesson on morality given by the Pastor, followed by an English lesson given by the mild-mannered, bespectacled Bible Student. The lessons were somewhat academic rather than useful, such as learning all the English words for 'cold', while the cross-eyed cook passed hours drawing up tremendous menus, taking his drooling listeners on tours of all the pubs and restaurants he had ever been to in his native city of Hamburg, introducing them with almost academic pedantry to new dishes with his usual opener:

'Now I know you will not believe me, but on the Waterfront they *do* eat a mixture of beans and pears…'

Despite the Bible Student's rigorous lesson plan, time

hung heavily on everyone's hands, and the hours between first parade at eight o'clock until the last one at five, before the sentries had their tea – 'Tea! If I ever hear that word again when I'm armed,' the air-gunner had threatened more than once, 'I'll shoot down the man who says it like a dog' – that time passed on leaden feet.

Otto, then, was not particularly surprised when on their second Saturday in the camp the wooden-faced air-gunner began to take very special care with his toilet. He took his second pair of pants from beneath his bunk to reveal a knife-edged crease, obtained by lining the inside with soap and sleeping on them. He shaved carefully, stropping the razor-blade with which they were issued once a month, on the inside of a drinking glass, and then completed his toilet by spraying his pubic hair with talcum powder.

'You never know who you might meet,' he said defiantly, seeing Otto's look.

'Yeah,' Otto said casually from his bunk, looking back to his Shakespearian sonnet that the Student had scribbled down from memory for Otto to learn. 'They tell me Greta Garbo is doing a tour of the camp this Saturday. She's supposed to go for blond blokes like you.'

The air-gunner made a certain suggestion.

'No can do, old friend,' Otto answered. 'Got a double-decker bus up there already.' And then, with another glance, 'I suppose you're going to the tea dance, eh?'

The air-gunner flushed slightly. 'I thought it might be a change,' he said defensively.

'Yes,' Otto remarked. 'Don't get caught, otherwise they might throw you in the Hole to cool off, without your tin of Vaseline!'

'Arse!' the air-gunner cursed and vanished with a new slight trembling of his buttocks, taut in the well-pressed pants, which Otto had not noticed until now.

'Yes, it definitely seems to be,' Otto agreed.

Otto wandered through the darkening camp, unable to settle down in the hut. The place seemed deserted; everyone was in the recreation hut, it appeared, enjoying the doubtful pleasures of the tea dancing.

He paused for a while and stared through the recreation hut's window at the flushed, excited faces, and the Italian accordionist on the stage, sweating heavily, as he provided the music for the dancing couples.

The air-gunner drifted by, waltzing with stiff, manly dignity in the arms of the Italian in the evening dress made of blackout curtain, who gazed up at him in dreamy admiration. Otto laughed shortly. 'Good job he used his talcum powder after all,' he said to himself and wandered on, his brow creased in a preoccupied frown.

What am I going to do? he asked himself, idly kicking at an empty tin. When he'd arrived here on that sunny morning in October, the decision to escape had been so easy to make. But even if he did manage to escape from the camp, where could he escape to?

England was an island, surrounded by sea. Where would he get a boat from? Hell, even if he did, how would he find Europe again? – He knew nothing about the sea and navigation. What had the little Camp commandant, who looked like an undersized monkey, said to them on the morning parade the previous day?

'Channel fog today, men. Europe cut off.' He had laughed at his own joke, the only one to do so, even after

Pastor Mueller had translated it yet once again. Now Otto knew what Captain Hawkins had meant. The continent of Europe was a long, long way off from this forgotten northern English city.

He dismissed the depressing thoughts from his mind and strolled through the growing October gloom. With the long Saturday evening stretching before him with absolutely nowhere to go and nothing to do (the Camp library consisted of *Mein Kampf*, the Bible and S*truwwelpeter*, illustrated, and he had no interest in any of the three). At York, there was no friendly pub, where he could be swallowed into its smoky noisy warmth, its zinc bar awash with beer suds. There was also no girlfriend to provide two hours of sweating, red-faced exertion in the hot darkness, fighting to cross that invisible frontier, the distance between the stocking top and the first exhilarating feel of knicker elastic; and no 'Kabarett' with its fantastically long-legged chorus girls in old-fashioned *pickelhausen* and black silk stockings and nothing much else, and honestly vulgar comedians who stopped drunken hecklers with the old crack, 'Oh, don't pay any attention to him, *meine Damen*, he's had an unhappy love affair. He's just broken his right hand, ha, ha!'

Otto cursed under his breath. A year ago, the thought of peacefully living out his war in a British POW camp might have seemed like a jolly good career decision. But now, after months of tedious touting to the troops in France, he had a yearning to return to his homeland, to a life of skulduggery and quick bucks with the odd mission thrown in by the Count. At this very moment he would have welcomed the Count – wherever he might be now – soutane, shovel-hat, crazy schemes and all, with open arms. Since their first meeting,

55

Otto had come to rely on the wacky gentleman as a companion in his adventuring. *I'd have escaped into England by now*, Otto thought, *if the Count was around to escape with.* Where the devil was he right now? Did he need Otto's help?

He needed to get out of this place.

It was just then that he caught sight of a familiar figure hobbling ahead of him in the thickening darkness. It was Pastor Mueller. But there was something peculiar about the fat Protestant priest. He was moving in a strange, stiff legged manner, dribbling something behind him onto the ground, as he did so. Had the pastor had an unfortunate accident, the thought flashed through Otto's mind. The 'chilled Yid' did have a rather precipitous effect on the bowels.

Pastor Mueller heard Otto's footsteps, just as the younger man realised what the stuff was that was trickling so strangely out of the bottom of the priest's right trouser-leg. It was soil!

Mueller turned and Otto could just see his gold-capped teeth gleam in a smile, as he recognised who was behind him. He relaxed and said, 'I thought you would be at the tea dancing, Herr Stahl?'

'No, I didn't fancy the – er – ladies.'

Pastor Mueller followed the direction of Otto's gaze and knew it was no use attempting to lie now. He said softly, 'Home or Homo by Christmas, Herr Stahl.'

CHAPTER 7

'I don't usually wear these bags,' Pastor Mueller said, as Otto stared at him in the gloom, wondering what he was talking about.

'You mean the trousers?'

'Yes. You see under my own, I have two legs chopped off a pair of woollen underpants – the nights are cold in York, I can tell you. The tops are tied to each end of a piece of string. I loop the string around my neck under my pullover and suspend the underpant legs that way inside my outer trousers.' He beamed at the completely bewildered Otto, who was still trying to make sense of his original cryptic remark, 'home or homo by Christmas'.

'I have a pin attached to a piece of string stuck in each inside bag, with the strings running into my trousers' pockets. As I walk – or hobble might be a better description, Herr Stahl – I let the soil loose that way in a steady trickle. Afterwards I walk back the way I've come and tread it into the surface of the earth.' He ground his foot down and around to illustrate his method. 'See, indistinguishable from the normal top soil.'

Otto had already realised that camp life quickly turned people slightly mad, and the plump priest had been the Tommies' prisoner since 1939 after all. Was he cracked, too? 'But why,' he managed to croak, 'why do you go around getting rid of soil like this, *Herr Pfarrer*?' He edged away from the beaming parson a little, just in case he was dangerous as well as crazy.

'Why?' Pastor Mueller chuckled and his jowls rumbled in the semi-darkness. 'Because I and a few other like-minded spirits are getting out.'

'Out?' Otto echoed. 'Out of here?'

'Yes, out of here. Out of England.'

'Christ!' ejaculated Otto.

'Shush, my boy,' the parson said hastily. 'You don't want the sentries to hear. Besides, I have reason to suspect that there is a Tommy spy in the camp.' He took Otto by the arm and made him start walking.

'You said out,' Otto whispered, while over at the recreation hut, the accordionist swung into *Solo Mio* and suddenly the night air was full of liquid Italian tenors, as someone opened the hut's windows and began to fix the blackout shutters.

'Get them sodding lights dowsed!' one of the sentries shouted roughly from a watch-tower. 'Lot of bloody macaroni pansies!'

Over at another of the stork-legged towers another sentry laughed and called, 'I don't know, Charlie. It's better than wanker's doom and going blind.'

'Who wants to be a pilot anyway?' Charlie called back mysteriously and laughed raucously.

Otto could hardly wait till the little exchange was over, questions jostling to be voiced in his youthful mind. 'You said out. Why? How? Do you have a plan?'

'One question at a time, my boy,' the plump parson replied calmly. 'Firstly, why? Because I have not wasted these last eighteen years in Hull ministering to drunken seamen in the Mission, only to be jailed at the first whiff of war. I've been up and down the Yorkshire and Humber coastline. I know it like the back of my hand. I have information that will be vital to our High Command when they invade England. I have no doubt they will reward me for my diligence. I rather fancy a pastorship in Hamburg's St Pauli. Very upper-class, you know.'

Otto said nothing. He had come to think of Mueller as an intelligent, like-minded, peace-loving gentleman. He hadn't realised how much of a die-hard this pastor actually was.

'Two: how will I escape? Through the Hole.'

'The Hole?' Otto repeated.

Pastor Mueller chuckled softly. 'Exactly. It's the building closest to the wire, and it's easy to get into. Why, to coin a phrase, it is as easy to gain entry to the Hole as it is for a sinner to go to Hell. Three, the big plan. Through the port of Hull. On the north-east coast,' he added for Otto's information. 'Some sixty kilometres from here.'

'I don't know it,' Otto said. 'But how will you get away from there, even if you do manage to break out of this place?'

'There is still a thriving trade between Hull and Sweden, Herr Stahl. Timber, steel, ball-bearings and the like. The Swedes are good businessmen – they sell to both us and the Tommies. And I know most of their sea captains. I've seen most of them carried into my Mission at one time or another for Sunday service. The Swedes are great churchgoers, and great drunks.' He chuckled. 'Well, Otto, I may call you by your first name?'

'Please do.'

'We of the escape committee have had you under

observation for the last week or so. We always do that with new people. First, for security reasons, and then to check out whether that person is the right type. We've already rejected that wooden-faced Luftwaffe chap. He has no talent for clandestine work whatsoever. He'd give the game away in a day.'

'Perhaps,' Otto agreed, wondering what was coming. 'I think he's got other things on his mind at the moment.'

'The cook is hopeless. Won't be able to stand the work, as for the Bible Student, I can't think he's in a hurry to get back to the Fatherland. I feel he'll be content to spend the rest of the war here, reciting his sonnets and reading the – er – Holy Word.'

Otto felt he detected a note of contempt in Pastor Mueller's voice, but it was too dark now to have his supposition confirmed by the look on the portly priest's face. 'You would think he'd get bored reading it,' he said. 'After all he does know the story.'

'Hm, yes, Otto. Well, as I said we've been watching you and you seem to fit the bill. You're strong, tight-lipped, and I have the feeling you want to get out of it.'

'You're right enough there, *Herr Pfarrer,*' he replied quickly. In reality, Otto's brain had already filled with images of British police shooting him in the back half way through a daring escape, British soldiers executing him in the line to board a boat, British farmwives sticking him through with pitchforks after finding him in their hay loft. He shivered.

Pastor Mueller laid his hand on Otto's shoulder in a fatherly manner. 'Good, then, I think you should be let into the secret. Come on, I'll take you into the Hole. They should be ready for a night's work by now.'

Otto followed him, as somewhere up in the darkness a guard lazily started whistling *We'll Meet Again*. From the other side of the compound, a voice shouted in English, 'Shut your trap, Vera! Or I'll have to come over there and shut it for you!'

'Incompetent Tommies,' Mueller whispered to Otto. 'We could be stealing the Crown Jewels from right under their noses and they wouldn't have any idea what was happening.'

The pastor was fumbling in his pocket for something. A second later Otto found out what it was. A key, which he inserted in the barred door of the punishment hut, saying, 'Made of the key from a sardine tin... makes a wonderful skeleton key.' He chuckled softly. 'It is amazing the things one learns to do behind prison bars. You know, my boy, I really do enjoy this criminal business, I really do.' Together they passed inside. 'Goodness knows what is going to become of me, if this goes on.'

'Goodness indeed!' Otto agreed, wondering whether he shouldn't just cut his losses right now and go straight back to bed. Thinking back, the hopes of escaping he'd had just a few minutes before seemed incredibly heroic. The wrong kind of heroic. The kind of heroic where every adventure ends in death by pitchfork and they award medals to your lifeless body.

'It's like this,' Hans, the pumper, said thickly, his naked upper body lathered with sweat as he pushed a dirty white kitbag in and out laboriously. 'If you were ever to see me with a tree trunk sticking out of my arse – forgive my French, *Herr Pfarrer* – don't stare. It's all part of the tunnel.'

Pastor Mueller smiled benevolently down at Hans, as he pumped at rough, home-made bellows and explained to an

61

open-mouthed Otto, 'Our Hans here supplies them with air, you see. The kitbag acts as a bellows. It sends the oxygen down the air lines. They're made of empty milk powder cans. Look,' he pointed to a rickety line of cans, each joint wrapped around tightly with newspaper, which led into the floor of the candle-lit Hole and disappeared somewhere below. 'The clean air goes down and the stale air, rising as it always does, comes out.'

'What, there are *people* down there?' Otto asked, horrified.

'Who else is going to build the shitting tunnel? Oh, excuse me, Pastor,' Hans gasped as he pushed and pulled the kitbag in and out like an enormous accordion, 'Sod it, how many times have I cursed the thing!'

'God will reward you, my son,' Pastor Mueller said mildly, obviously unaffected by the big, bald-headed seaman's rough language.

'I wouldn't mind a little reward in the here-and-now.'

Pastor Mueller chuckled, obviously highly pleased with himself for some reason or other. 'I should think that could be arranged.' He looked directly at Otto. 'You look a strong young fellow, Otto. Do you think you could manage Hans's job?'

Otto looked from the priest to the sweating seaman and said cautiously, 'I suppose so. Why do you ask?'

'Because Otto,' Mueller said carefully. 'We've got diggers down there enough, but we want someone with real stamina for the pump.'

Otto's heart was racing. This was dangerous. If he said yes, he'd be absolutely committing himself to this loony scheme. Someone would no-doubt start shooting at him in the not too distant future. 'And if I refuse?' he asked.

Mueller's smile vanished. 'Then, my dear Otto, I'm afraid we couldn't let you walk away and blab out our little secret after a few too many mugs of that rotgut potato schnapps some of the Italians make in their kitchen.'

'What do you mean?'

'I'll tell you,' the sweating Hans grunted. 'In zero-comma-nothing seconds, you'd be planted down there,' he indicated what Otto now knew was the entrance to an escape tunnel, 'looking at the tatties from below – for good. He looked hard at the newcomer. Out of the corner of his eye, the young, blond, well-toned Otto could see that Pastor Mueller had the same lethal, menacing look on his face too. He felt a cold finger of fear trace its length along the small of his back. They weren't fooling, he knew that instinctively. *What a tits-up,* he thought. *Say no, get knifed. Say yes, get pitchforked.*

Pastor Mueller laughed, but there was no joy in that laugh as he stood there in the chill corridor, with the gasp-gasp of the pump the only sound and the candles flickering eerily in the draught that came from below. 'A louse ran over your liver, I suppose, eh?'

'Yes,' Otto agreed, his mind racing now.

'Well, my dear Otto, what is it to be? We cannot afford to waste any more time. The nights are too short.'

Otto gulped. 'I'm... with you,' he said with difficulty.

Pastor Mueller smiled. 'I thought somehow you would be,' he remarked mildly. He stuck out his hand. 'Welcome to the York Tunnel Company Limited!'

Numbly Otto took the hand and pressed it slightly, wondering just what he had let himself in for now.

'You start tomorrow evening, Otto,' the priest said

softly. 'Now you'd better get back to your hut before any of the perverts see you. Good night.'

'Good night.' His gaze flicked from Mueller to the sweating Hans, still pumping at the bellows.

Otto walked out into the night in a daze, telling himself it just seemed impossible for him to escape the war. Try as he might, the bloody thing always caught up with him.

On the towers the bored, cynical English sentries were making kissing sounds, by sucking the backs of their hands, and in the silver shadows cast by the ascending moon, there were soft whispers like Otto remembered lovers making in better days. He shivered. 'Home or Homo by December,' the pastor had said. How right he had been.

That night the air-gunner sneaked back into the hut long after the clock on the tower of the *Terry's* chocolate factory, which lay a kilometre or so away from the Camp, had struck two.

A wide-awake Otto could hear him sobbing softly to himself for a long time on the bunk above. *That's what you get for jumping into bed with the wrong crowd*, he thought, ironically.

CHAPTER 8

The tunnellers met each Sunday morning 'for the service' in the little recreation hut. To anyone else in the camp, it would look like a traditional service for the particularly devout, as camp-wide prayers would be over by then. Once, the Bible student wandered in, but was swiftly shooed away by the Pastor with, 'We don't want your kind in here, with those radical doctrines of yours. We practise good, old-fashioned honest religion here, clear!'

It was during his first 'service' the next morning that Otto met his fellow tunnellers for the first time.

They were all old hands like Mueller, ten in all. There was Kraemer, for instance, a giant, whose muscles bulged brutally through his tunic, who had been captured in Narvik in April 1940. Todt, a skinny *Wehrmacht* corporal, who had been captured blind-drunk in a French *estaminet* during a local English counter-attack back in June.

But whatever their arm of the service – and they came from all three branches – they all believed fervently in the National Socialist cause and in a swift victory for German arms when they would return to a hated England, that had imprisoned them, as important personages.

As Hans, the pumper, whose destroyer had been sunk by a British submarine in the Channel, said thickly, 'One day

I'm gonna be *Gauleiter* and then I'll make those god-damn buck-teethed Tommies jump through the shitting hoop – excuse my French, *Herr Pfarrer* – that I will!'

But it was Pastor Mueller who was the tunnellers' undoubted leader, in spite of his mild, benevolent manner and the fact that he never did any of the work in the tunnel – 'too weak for the pumps and too smart to be caught with you lot of crooks below ground,' he was wont to say with that crooked smile of his. Somehow Otto knew that Pastor Mueller was dangerous, very dangerous indeed.

Soon, he would find out just how right he was.

On any given Sunday the men would receive their tasks and orders for the week, for Pastor Mueller thought it dangerous for them to meet together on any other day of the week, and thus it was that as soon as the tea-time roll-call was finished, each man, armed with one of the sardine-can skeleton keys, would sneak into the Hole, and begin the evening's labour, urged on by a beaming, fat-bellied Pastor Mueller softly singing the popular song of the day, 'Hi, ho, hi, ho, it's off to work we go!' from the film Snow White and the Seven Dwarfs: a song which usually occasioned one of the tunnellers to snap, 'Well, he bloody well don't look like Snow White to me!'

By the time Otto joined the *York Tunnelgesellschaft GmbH*, the tunnel had progressed some twenty metres towards the fence. It had been dug solely by improvised scoops and picks and the odd garden tool that they had found around the camp before the commandant had ordered all such implements to be removed.

The tunneller worked sitting, hacking away at the clay-and-soil mix of that depth, digging out a third of a metre of the stuff at a time before pausing to shore up the whole structure with bed boards stolen from bunks in empty huts, making a little box-like structure some one metre high and one metre broad. This done, he would add another couple of cans to the air-pipe trailing behind him, pack the links with paper, and commence the process all over again by the flickering yellow light of a candle resting on a saucer at his side. It was hard, back-breaking work and none of the tunnellers could stand it longer than half an hour, not even the giant Kraemer; and all of them clambered up out of the entrance which lay in the passage between the cells of the Hole, complaining of dizziness and headaches, due to the foul air.

But it wasn't easy for Otto either, taking turns with the balding Hans, pushing and pulling the makeshift bellows rhythmically so that cool fresh air from beneath the Hole surged into the tunnel and forced the black fumes from the candles in wisps out of the entrance in a steady stream. By the end of an hour, his shoulder muscles afire, sweat streaming down into his eyebrows and blinding him, he would be counting off the seconds until it was time for an invariably grumpy Hans to take over the task and he could rest his burning muscles.

Promptly at midnight, the pastor would call a halt. Up would come the weary, dirt-covered tunnellers and thereupon all of them, pumpers and tunnellers, would load up with the freshly excavated earth to be disposed of by the same means as the priest had used on the Saturday that Otto had first become aware of the escape plan. Hastily the great grey-coloured heavy slab of concrete was placed over the entrance to the tunnel, damp bread pushed into the cracks around it to resemble mortar, and dust sprinkled over it from the can that

Mueller always had with him – 'sometimes I feel like a priest giving out holy water,' he often joked – so that it looked as if it had not been disturbed since the last time somebody had thought to make a prisoner sweep it.

Furtively they would steal across the blacked-out compound to the pastor's room – as senior man, he had a hut to himself – where they would remove all traces of their night's work, even picking fingernails clean, while the rest of the POWs snored in their bunks, unaware of what was going on.

But although most of them were desperately tired after the unaccustomed hard labour on the poor food, the pastor would not let them leave for their own bunks until he was personally satisfied that they were 'clean', as he called it. 'You must remember,' he lectured them severely more than once, 'that security is vital. One slip up – er I believe that is the phrase you crooks use, isn't it – and we're sunk. I trust the Macaroni as far as I can throw them and their perverted boyfriends even less. Any one of them would betray us to the Tommies for the sake of a lipstick or a pair of stockings.'

'Let me catch one of the lace-knickered warm-brothers trying anything,' Kraemer, the giant, would growl, twisting his hairy paws as if he were wringing some poor Italian's neck, 'and he won't be talking much longer.'

Pastor Mueller would nod his agreement and on such occasions the mild, benevolent look would be absent from his eyes behind the gold-rimmed spectacles. Otto knew that the bunch of them were not just making idle talk. They would deal harshly with any traitor; there was no doubt about that. Otto started to worry. He was back in the company of Nazis, whose philosophy of life he hated. They were men who were part of the system he had tried so hard to avoid so that he did not have to serve it.

As October gave way to November and the tunnel progressed steadily forward and ever closer to the wire, Otto Stahl began to ponder how he might use *York Tunnelgesellschaft GmbH* to his own advantage.

In the first week of December 1940, with the weather in the north now really becoming cold, heralding the hard winter to come, the pastor ordered the shoring system to be changed to save wood. Somehow the Italians had found a way to enter the empty locked huts too and were stealing the wood from the bunks: the tunnellers would have to use less. Now, instead of solid frame all the way, they spaced the boards at thirty-centimetre intervals and laid single boards on top to hold the roof soil up.

Immediately they started having roof falls and hardly an evening passed without work having to stop to allow some unfortunate, choking tunneller to be dragged out and laid on the floor above in the corridor fighting for breath like a drowning man.

All this was just after Otto had volunteered for tunnel-digging duty. He had had enough of the pump and the tunnellers only did half-hour shifts. The pastor did not object and for a while at least Todt the shifty-looking corporal, was glad enough to take over his place at the pump-bellows.

With the new system of shoring, the tunnel had to be dug forward for nearly a metre before a box frame could be erected and the roof be lined and Otto quickly realised that no matter how carefully he attempted to scrape the arch of earth above him out, it virtually always cracked and fell in. Time and time again, he heard the cracking noise of the soil giving way and managed to duck backwards out of the way of the miniature landslide. But even then the airline was virtually always blocked and it would be left gasping there, shocked and choking for breath, in the stinking darkness, for the candle invariably went out. Still, he told himself, it was better than the bellows, with Hans and the pastor watching him all the time, as if they still did not quite trust him.

It gave him time to think too, for down there in the flickering semi-darkness, half-naked and lathered in sweat, he was alone, and he felt he needed that solitude if he were going to think out some solution to his ever-present problem: how was he going to escape and at the same time get rid of the others?

For now they were getting ever closer to the wire and already at their 'Sunday services' there was excited talk of preparing escape equipment, the bits and pieces of hoarded civilian clothes they would wear, the amount of food they should hoard from their meagre rations, with the pastor making one of his usual theological jokes when they asked for further details of the neutral Swedish ships that would bear them away:

'Faith is all you need, comrades. As the Good Book says, "Thou shalt have faith and walk upon the waters".' To which Hans had answered grumpily, 'I'd prefer to do it in a nice big fat freighter, thank you very much, *Herr Pfarrer*.'

It was in the week before Christmas – with Italians, egged on by excited 'boyfriends', already beginning to dress up in female finery for the festive concert they had promised to give – that it all started.

Otto was working a particularly loose section of tunnel,

his head half turned, ears cocked for the slightest sound of cracking earth, when it happened. Without any warning, the roof gave in and he was buried in well over a hundred pounds of earth, gasping and spluttering and terribly frightened down in the pitch black.

It took the others nearly an hour to free him and bring him round again, with Pastor Mueller trying to soothe then-rattled nerves with one of his mild theological jokes, saying as Otto finally sat up and cleared the rest of the earth from his eyes, 'They do say that the "meek shall inherit the earth".'

'Well, I inherited my share of it for tonight,' Otto gasped grimly.

'Yes, I suppose, you have. All of us have,' the fat priest agreed, looking at his wrist-watch. 'It is about time that we all packed up for the night. We can clear the fall tomorrow evening.'

Thus it was that Otto returned to his hut earlier than usual. Physically and emotionally exhausted, he flopped down on his bunk, not noticing the couple locked in each other's arms in the silver gloom. A minute later he was fast asleep and snoring softly, while the air-gunner, in need of a pre-sleep pee, prized himself away from his personal sleeping beauty and tiptoed past. Pushing Otto's discarded boots to one side in the latrine, a soft whistle escaped his lips. Mud was falling from the soles, a completely different colour to that found outside in the compound: a light yellow instead of the dark-brown of the soot-dirtied soil found everywhere in York. *Well, Kurt you old cock,* he told himself, *one doesn't need to be particularly clever to know why*. So that was what his fellow prisoner had been doing out so late at night!

***

'It's Renate the Red-Hot Mama from Milano,' Staff-Sergeant Dicks announced softly. 'She, er, he's got something to tell you sir.'

Captain Hawkins, standing at the window of his office staring outside at the first soft snowflakes of the winter falling on the roofs of York Camp, turned round swiftly and said, 'Wheel it in, Dicksey.'

A moment later the Italian came swishing in, trailing the long gown he was going to wear at the Christmas concert behind him with affected elegance, face heavy with powder, two hectic spots of rouge at the cheeks, as if he were suffering from an advanced stage of consumption.

'*Comniandante, que dice?*' he simpered, rolling his mascaraed eyes provocatively. '*Querido,*' he pursed his lips and blew the wizened little ex-quartermaster a wet kiss.

'Oh come on, don't screw about,' Hawkins said testily although he was always amused by Capaldi's performance. 'You know we've got to get you in and out of here smartish.'

'Gimme a quick pint, and I'll tell you,' the Italian said in a broad West Yorkshire accent and plumped down heavily on Hawkins's chair, 'I'm fair clem!'

Hawkins nodded to Dicks, who was guarding the door, as he always did when their own private stool-pigeon came to make his weekly report. Hurriedly he opened the steel drawer marked 'entertainment' and finding a bottle of Bass Ale handed it to the Italian.

Capaldi bit off the cap with his teeth, spat it out and drunk deep of the warmish beer, then belched with pleasure and said, 'Drop o' grand stuff that. God knows how those wops can drink all that red wine muck!'

'Well?' Hawkins said expectantly. 'Come on Capaldi,

cough it up, lad.'

Capaldi, the son of an ice-cream dealer in Bradford, who had gone for a holiday back to Italy in 1939, had been called up for the Italian Army and had been captured in Libya the following year, said, his made-up face serious now:

'They've got a tunnel somewhere, the Squareheads. Anyway that's what my boyfriend Kurt thinks. He doesn't know where exactly or who's in the escape team, but they've definitely got one.' He drained the rest of the beer and, hitching up his skirt, added, 'And tell my old man to send over a crate of ale for Boxing Day, 'cos I'm really gonna get pissed then.'

'I will,' Captain Hawkins promised, 'and watch out for yerself, laddie.'

'That I will, *Signor Commandante*,' the little Italian queer trilled. 'But who'd want to harm me – with my beautiful behind? *Ciao*.'

He sailed out back to the compound, leaving Dicks and Hawkins staring at each other in gloomy silence. Their safety relied on keeping these prisoners inside that fence.

'What cheek,' the Commandant exclaimed. 'After everything we've done for the buggers! Giving them leniency, allowing their late night parties, their music... And still they want to leave. Are they mad? And just when Christmas is coming up, Dicksey. I thought they liked it here.' He slumped back in his wooden office chair. 'It's time to stop playing the benevolent father.'

CHAPTER 9

It happened on the day when the preparations for Christmas were reaching their high point. In the primitive kitchens, the prisoners, who had saved their raisins and sugar rations for weeks, were busy making 'raisin wine'.

For days they had been boiling the raisins and sugar in the issue cauldrons, draining the sludge through towels until now they were slowly achieving the final product: raisin wine with a fantastic alcoholic kick.

In the recreation hut, ten Italians, dressed as can-can girls, complete with padded brassieres, black stockings and suspenders, were practising the climax of their act – the splits – with disastrous results on their precious silken knickers, while in the other comer a grim-faced disapproving group of tunnellers were going through '*Stille Nachte, Heilige Nacht,*' once again with ponderous Germanic thoroughness. Everywhere there was hustle and bustle, the sound of sawing and hammering, interspersed by excited little cries from the Southern Italians every time fresh snowflakes came tumbling down, for most of them had never seen snow before. Crying '*que bella,*' some of them even applauded, as if God himself was putting on a special act to entertain them this Christmas so far from their Sicilian homeland.

Abruptly the main gate was flung open. Whistles

shrilled. On their towers the sentries swung round their Bren guns to train them directly on the compound. Three heavy lorries came roaring into the compound at low gear and started careering around between the huts, their backs laden with bricks. Captain Hawkins, followed by a dozen guards, helmeted and with fixed bayonets, came running through the snow at the double. In a flash they were inside the nearly empty huts, flinging aside bedding, poking their bayonets into gaps in the wooden walls, throwing down the prisoners' pathetic bits and pieces of kit from the cupboards and rummaging through them like jostling housewives fighting to find a bargain at a jumble sale.

In an instant all was angry, excited confusion, all thoughts of Christmas gone, as the choir, the can-can chorus, the wine-makers were herded into the snow for a personal search, which left the Germans sullen and angry, the queers who formed the can-can group flashing-eyed and excited, and the Tommies who had searched them red faced with embarrassment. One of the Italians even had the audacity to blow a kiss at the Commandant, who promptly ordered him seven days in the Hole.

'Bloody saucy bugger,' he snapped, as the unrepentant Italian was led away roughly, his right suspender broken and his black stocking drooping around his ankle. 'There's no plum duff for that dago this Christmas!'

The search continued for another two hours, with soldiers in khaki overalls who wore the cap badge of the Royal Engineers and didn't belong to the Camp's establishment, crawling beneath the huts, listening to the floors with stethoscopes like crazy doctors and running long metal rods through the snow and into the ground below to withdraw and examine the ends excitedly.

Just before midday, they gave up, for they could already hear the rattle of the dixies over at their own cookhouse and the scent of fried bully was flooding the compound by now. It was Friday and there was rice pudding for 'afters' on Fridays; it was the culinary treat of the week. The Brits' enthusiasm waned rapidly. Sour-faced and still angry, Captain Hawkins put his revolver back into his holster.

'All right Staff Sergeant Dicks,' he snapped, 'withdraw the jaiwans, there's nothing doing here!'

'Withdraw the what, sir?'

'The soldiers – *squaddies,*' Hawkins cried angrily, frustrated by the fact they had found nothing in spite of his well-laid plan to surprise the POWs. 'Christ man, don't you speak English?'

And with that he strode off out of the compound, muttering terrible oaths to himself in Urdu, leaving an offended Staff Sergeant Dicks to withdraw the hungry jaiwans.

That afternoon Pastor Mueller held a 'special pre-Christmas service' in his own quarters, but there was nothing festive or Christian about it. Mueller was white-faced with anger, while the mood of the other 'worshippers' varied from sadistic to homicidal.

'It all adds up, comrades,' he launched straight into his own analysis. 'They know we've got a tunnel going. Why else would they need those heavy trucks?'

'Yer,' Hans agreed, 'and loads of bricks on the back to make them even heavier. They were trying to cave in any tunnel they'd run over.' He gave a short, sour grunt. 'Those buck-teethed Tommies'll have to get up earlier in the morning, if they're gonna find our tunnel–'

'Yer and those other Tommies with their probes and stupid rubber hearing-aids,' Todt said. 'They were after our tunnel too!'

Mueller held up his hands for silence. 'Let me say this fast, comrades. From now onwards we no longer speak of tunnels. The word will no longer be used even among ourselves. I have a code word for it which we will from this moment on employ in reference to it. Now it will be called *Adolf.*' He gave them a little smile. 'The name of our beloved *Führer*, of course.'

There was a slight round of applause and someone said, 'I don't know, *Herr Pfarrer*, but you certainly do come up with some brilliant ideas.'

Oh shit on the shingle, Otto cursed to himself at the sudden looks of delight on the faces of his companions. *Brilliant, my arse!* But he said nothing, waiting for what Mueller would have to say next.

The priest's smile vanished. 'Comrades, the situation is serious, very serious.' He wet his bottom lip and now for the first time, Otto noticed just how thick and very red it was – it was the lip of a sensualist. 'It is clear that the Tommies didn't just come in here by chance. Not in the morning, they didn't. We all know the Tommies never really get started until they've read their *Daily Mirror* properly and had their mid-morning tea-break.'

There was a rumble of agreement from the others.

'No, comrades, never, unless it was something serious. And this was serious enough to get them moving early. They knew the tunnel – excuse me – Adolf is there. How?' He paused dramatically. '*Because Adolf was betrayed!*'

The effect was that of an 88mm shell exploding. Men jumped to their feet. Others struck their temples like characters in a Greek tragedy miming utter despair. Others gasped, as if they had been punched in the solar plexus. Only Otto showed no emotion whatsoever, for he noticed with a chill feeling that Pastor Mueller was staring directly at him, seemingly unaffected by the impact of his own announcement.

The noise and confusion seemed to go on for a long time until finally Pastor Mueller raised his hands high like a boxing referee declaring a knock-out, and said, 'Comrades... comrades! Please, we mustn't be carried away.'

Slowly, order was restored and everyone looked expectantly at the fat priest, while outside the snowflakes fell sadly and the Italian accordionist attempted to play Jingle Bells, but failed miserably, the Christmas song sounding very much like the tangoes he usually played.

'In the hours since the search, comrades, I have done a great deal of thinking,' the pastor continued. 'Who? I have asked myself, "Who," time and time again, comrades. Who. Who would... could betray Adolf in such a *dastardly* fashion?' He raised his gaze to the ceiling, drunk on his own evangelising. 'Who?'

Oh, get on with it, you stupid shit, Otto said to himself, in an aggressive outburst brought on by the rising tide of fear in his stomach. And now, as had happened so awkwardly before, he could feel a bulging of his pants down below. 'Goddamit!' he cursed under his breath.

'I have considered every one of you, comrades, I must admit that,' Mueller added over the shocked intakes of breath from the congregation. 'After all we are but Mortal Men, exposed to the Temptations of the Flesh – even more than normally in the case of this hellish camp. All of us have experienced the Dark Night of the Soul at one time or other, in which we could well have strayed from the Straight and Narrow Path, save for the assistance of our Maker Himself.' Automatically he bowed his balding head and clasped his hands together, as if in prayer. Otto could have sworn he heard him mutter 'Amen'.

'However, comrades,' now there was nothing sanctimonious about Mueller's voice when he resumed speaking, 'we're not that kind of swine. None of us here would indulge in that form of swinery.' His eyes flashed angrily.

'Then who was it?' Hans asked.

'One of the new men,' Mueller declared flatly. 'The Macaronis are fools. They know nothing. But our own so-called German *comrades*,' he emphasized the word with a sneer, 'they know everything, or think they do.'

'Which one of them?' Kraemer growled, and Otto sat transfixed by the strangling movements he was making with his great hairy paws. 'Just tell me and I'll see he passes on right quick.' He guffawed at his own attempt at humour. 'Get that *Herr Pfarrer* – passes on?'

'Yes, yes,' Mueller said hastily. 'In all there are four of them, Otto here who has worked hard with us on Adolf for the last few weeks, the Bible student, the cook from Hamburg, and Kurt the air-gunner.' He paused significantly while the others waited expectantly. 'I have thought about them and have come to this conclusion,' he continued finally.

'The Bible student,' he ticked him off on one fat finger. 'A dreamer, a fool, but an honest fool, who can't see beyond the end of his long, sharp nose. For him the world ended two thousand years ago.' Otto frowned. It seemed a strange statement to be coming from a parson, he told himself.

'The cook!' Mueller continued.

'Oh that fat sod!' Todt said contemptuously. 'He can't see anything but the end of his own greasy guts.'

'Agreed, Todt. His sole interest in this life is food and food yet once again. So that leaves Otto here – and the air-gunner.'

Suddenly Otto was aware they were all staring at him and that their eyes were heavy with menace. He moved his left hand to cover the towering erection he couldn't control. He raised his right, as if he were about to push them away physically.

'Now come off it,' he said with a shaky laugh. 'I'm not your traitor. I want to get out as much as you lot do. Honest!'

The priest let Otto suffer, obviously enjoying his discomfiture in that somewhat threatening atmosphere. Otto glanced around at the group of wild-eyed, Nazi-loving nutcases. Shifty-looking Todt had taken out a shiv and was fingering the blade. The bulging eyes of Kraemer belied barely-controlled aggression. Hans looked like he was imagining pummelling something other than the bellows for once.

And then Mueller said, 'Don't worry, Otto. It's not you! It's the air-gunner.'

Another round of gasps and cries from the assembled.

'The swine!' Hans declared hotly, his anger immediately directed away from Otto, who could feel a great weight lifting off his chest, and pressure relieving itself below. Hans was talking: 'But how do you know, *Herr Pfarrer*?'

81

'Intuition, Hans,' Mueller declared and tapped the side of his long nose knowingly. 'Intuition.'

'So when do we kill the little shit?' Kraemer growled.

Otto gasped. 'Kill him – in the camp?' he exclaimed. 'But we're prisoners, aren't we?'

Mueller looked at him coldly. 'Are we?' he asked. 'Who is the prisoner and who is the guard, eh?' He turned to the others. 'But first of all, he must have a trial – and *then* we kill him.'

'Democracy in action,' Otto commented sardonically. But no one was listening to Otto any more.

'When – where?' several voices demanded hastily, drowning Otto's words.

'Tomorrow night.'

'But that's Christmas Eve,' Todt objected.

'So?' Mueller said and then smiled, though there was no humorous light in his faded eyes behind the gold-rimmed glasses. 'It'll be a Christmas present for him to remember.'

The others laughed uproariously, save Otto, whose mind was racing wildly. What was he going to do?

CHAPTER 10

'Jesus bloody wept!' Captain Hawkins moaned, rubbing his thinning hair in despair, 'I'm going to the dogs, right stoically; knocking back the sherab as if it were water, smoking a bloody ration of coffin-nails a day and not even able to get the old John Thomas up at night!'

'Is it the tunnel, sir?' Staff-Sergeant Dicks asked a little helplessly, while outside the office the snow fell in solid white sheets, and some sentry or other sang in a monotonous, mournful voice, '*Kiss me goodnight, Sar'nt-Major. Tuck me in my little wooden bed. We all love you, Sar'nt-Major.*'

'I'll have that janker-wallah out there in the nick if he doesn't stop that bleeding howling in half a mo,' Hawkins groaned. 'Of course it's the tunnel, you silly sod!'

'But we did try,' Dicks said.

'Ay, but not hard enough, that's the trouble. At this very moment, the squarehead buggers might well be burying their way through the earth right beneath our plates of meat! God, it gets right up my nose! I've tried to pump their mullah, that Parson Mueller, but the fat old sky pilot's not letting on, if he knows anything. I've even offered them bribes, but those sods know nothing, and even Capaldi, the fairy-queen, hasn't come up with anything new from his boyfriend, the silly poofter!'

As if on cue the unknown singer outside broke off his mournful account of his love for the 'Sar'nt-Major' and launched into a lively rendition of '*Tight as a drum, never been done, queen of all the fairies. She's only one titty to feed the baby on!*'

Exasperated beyond all measure Captain Hawkins opened the window with a curse and bellowed into the snowstorm, 'That man out there! Stop that sodding howling down there or I'll have you on jankers from now to the day yer get yer old-aged pension!'

'*Oh poor little bugger, he's only got one udder...*' The song trailed away to nothing and Captain Hawkins slammed the window closed, and turned back, his face white with snow.

'Too much bloody singing these days,' he grumbled. 'We didn't sing out in India in the old days. It's all this ruddy "Workers' Playtime" and Vera Lynn on about them sodding "White Cliffs of Dover".'

Then he remembered the problem in hand once again.

'Looky here, Dicksey,' he said, his voice more reasonable now. 'We've got to do something. 'Cos if we don't and some of the squareheads do a bunk, you'll know what will happen? It'll be back to the battalion and a nice swift posting to Libya to get yer knees brown right sharpish – and blokes are getting killed dead out there, even by the wogs!'

'Don't say things like that, sir,' Staff-Sergeant Dicks quavered and clutched the officer's desk, as if he might well faint. 'I ain't feeling too well as it is this morning. Me and my widow-woman had a proper night of it.'

'Yer typical, out fornicating while I'm eating my heart out here worrying, worrying,' Hawkins moaned. 'I know it in my bones. There's gonna be trouble. I knew it in Quetta just before the earthquake. I knew it in France just before the balloon went up last May. And I've got the same feeling here, Dicksey.' He stared grimly at the pudgy-faced NCO, with the dark blue circles under his eyes. 'We're in for trouble. It's gonna be a right old sodding Christmas, take it from me.'

The prisoners' Christmas Eve entertainment had gone exceedingly well despite the freezing cold outside and the meagre rations the Commandant had allowed them for the two-day holiday. 'Sod' em,' he'd told the sergeant-cook when the latter had asked about special Christmas rations. 'If they're gonna do a bunk, they're not having their guts full of my plum duff!' But the potent raisin wine had helped to overcome both the cold and lack of food.

The 'lovelies' of the Italian chorus-line had performed well to the accompaniment of delighted little cries and jeers of 'Don't split yer knickers, missus!' from their audience when they did the final splits.

The accordionist had succeeded in getting even the members of the *York Tunnelgesellschaft GmbH*, as hard-bitten as they were, to join in the community singing, though his rendition of '*O Solo Mio*' had reduced the Italian section of his audience to tears and there had been much blowing of noses and furtive wiping of eyes from them.

Now it was the Germans' turn. The light of the entertainment hut had been extinguished to cries of 'kiss me quick' and 'get your hand from under me skirt, you naughty man,' and the precious candles on the Christmas tree lit one by one to illuminate the German faces as they grouped around it, awaiting the pastor's orders, while the Italians stared in open-mouthed wonder at their transformed comrades; for now the hard-bitten faces were animated by that hazy Germanic *gemutlichkeit*, their eyes shining sentimental and childlike in the reflected light.

A beaming Pastor Mueller, standing just in front of the tree, nodded benignly to Todt, the shifty-eyed corporal, and he and the choir burst into '*Stille Nacht*' in fine full-voiced style, followed by '*Oh, Tannenbaum*' with the priest making pretty little movements with his entwined fingers to indicate they should keep their voices low. Politely the Italians clapped and waited to see what would happen next.

Kraemer, his hair sleeked down with Vaseline, his broad tough face awkward and red with embarrassment, stumbled forward through the choir, a piece of paper in his hand.

The pastor nodded and he started to read the poem, written laboriously on it, mumbling his words occasionally and hesitating over the bigger ones, all about 'homeland' and being on 'foreign soil', away from 'hearth and home and the loved ones.' All around, those Italians who spoke some German attempted to answer their comrades' enquiries of '*quedice, quediceil*,' while Otto shook his head in mock wonder. Only a German could be transformed from a ruthless, brutal, potential killer into a meek, wet-eyed sentimentalist who was prepared to read that kind of drivel in front of a shaggy tree hung with candles. He took a hefty drink of his raisin wine.

Finally it was over and with his hands clasped together in front of his portly belly in a very professional manner, Pastor Mueller commenced his little Christmas Eve speech, customary on such occasions back in the Reich, his voice low and vibrant and full of trained inspiration.

'Comrades,' he said, 'it is a sad thing to be away from one's loved ones on a day like this. It is an even sadder thing to be parted from them behind prison bars in a foreign land.'

His voice rose professionally.

'But comrades, years will come, when we and our beloved *Führer* Adolf Hitler have achieved final victory, when we will look back at this Christmas Eve of the year 1940 and remember it with quiet pride as a time of adversity over which we triumphed... because we were German and bear a German heart which is Good, True and Brave. We have been felled low, comrades, we have been beaten to our knees. Yet,' he raised one pudgy finger to emphasize his point, 'yet, the enemy has not succeeded in crushing us into the earth, in spite of his terrorist methods, such as not giving us any of his celebrated English plum pudding.'

He took off his glasses and wiped them hastily with his tie, almost as if he were too overcome by emotion to continue. 'We do not need his bribes, his alms, his plum pudding. We Germans need nothing on this earth, save the loyalty of a good brave comrade and the knowledge that our *Führer* Adolf Hitler,' he raised his eyes upwards piously, as if the *Führer* were floating slightly above his balding pate, 'is watching over us. That is all,' he finished, a little flatly.

Someone gave a sob. Kraemer reached hastily for his handkerchief and patted his eyes. Todt burst spontaneously into *Deutschland uber Alles*, followed almost instantly by the rest of the choir. A little startled and puzzled, yet caught up by the stirring spirit of that moment, the Italian chorus snapped to attention, their little skirts riding up to reveal their precious frilly knickers once again, and cried, '*Heil Hitler... Heil!*'

I am in the mad house, thought Otto.

Thirty minutes later as a slightly tipsy air-gunner staggered out of the entertainment hut humming the *Horst Wessel Lied* between repeated belches occasioned by the raisin wine, a powerful arm crooked itself around his throat to stop him from crying out aloud, and a hoarse brutal voice said from the cover of the raging snowstorm. 'All right, you treacherous arsehole. Now you're for it!'

At first, Kurt the air-gunner, the raisin wine still lending him courage, blustered, denying everything, shouting at his accusers with honest indignation. But, as the effects of the alcohol started to wear off, he began to falter, his features paling with fear as he realised that the hard-faced men staring at him in the candlelit priest's hut, with the storm howling outside drowning any cries he might make, were deadly serious.

Pastor Mueller let him go on for about five minutes before nodding to Kraemer, the one who had brought him in. With casual, effortless brutality, the giant hit the air-gunner in the stomach and as he doubled up with a frantic gasp, clubbed his fist down at the back of the Luftwaffe man's neck. He dropped to the ground sobbing with pain.

'How did you find out?' asked Mueller, softly.

Kraemer kicked him routinely in the ribs.

'The boots,' he sobbed, 'Otto's boots... There was clay on them... different from the surface earth.'

'*Damn!*' Mueller cursed himself, and snapped his fingers together angrily. 'We always forgot that one. Go on. What did you tell the Tommies?'

'I didn't tell–'

His words ended in a cry of pain, as Kraemer slapped

him open-handed and he slammed against the wall, gasping like a dying fish stranded out of water.

'Don't lie to me, you wretch!' Mueller thundered suddenly, half-rising from his chair with rage. 'For God's sake, man, if nothing else, think of your Immortal Soul.'

'But I didn't tell them anything,' Kurt mumbled through thickened, bloody lips, spitting out a little scarlet blood as he did so. 'Honest... on my word of honour.'

There was a quick outburst of gruff, disbelieving laughter and the prisoner stared wildly around those hard-faced men, knowing that he would find no sympathy there.

'It was the Eyeties then?' Todt suggested.

'Yer, your lace-knickered boyfriend,' Hans simpered in an affected falsetto.

'I might have mentioned it to Renate... trying to make myself seem a little bit important. They're impressed by such things. But that was all. Please believe me, all!'

Otto swallowed hard, as he watched the proceedings with horrified, sickened fascination, and told himself that they would have no mercy on the air-gunner; they hated him more than they did their captors, the Tommies.

Mueller took control hastily once again.

'Comrades, please,' he said. 'Let us get this unpleasant business over with as quickly as possible. I have something of vital importance to tell you in a few minutes!' He stared at the trembling, bleeding air-gunner. 'You could have destroyed the work of months,' he said harshly. 'You are a traitor – either by omission or commission, it matters not now. All that matters now is that you should be punished. As a warning to others of like mind.'

'Punished?' the air-gunner croaked, looking from one

89

hard face to the other, his own features a mixture of fear, fright, and disbelief. 'You are prisoners yourselves, how can you punish me?'

Mueller ignored the question. He rose slowly and solemnly to his feet. Automatically the others did the same, knowing now that the die was cast. Hans gave Otto a dig in the ribs and he did the same.

'Prisoner,' Mueller intoned, 'you are a disgrace to your service, your country and yourself. I find you guilty – and the Sentence is Death!'

'Death!' the air-gunner cried aghast. 'You mean murder!' he shrank back fearfully, hands outstretched as if to ward them off. 'You want to kill me!'

Mueller shook his head. 'No, we won't kill you. You will do that yourself.' He nodded to Kraemer. The giant produced a short length of stout rope from his jacket and said, 'The latrine is high enough to do it. One of the nancy-boys managed it very well last month.'

The air-gunner clutched his throat, as if he could already feel the hempen rope digging into his flesh. 'Why… why should I?' he gasped. 'You can't make me… If you want to kill me, you'll have to–'

'A letter to your parents, to the authorities, to your girl, if you have one,' Mueller said remorselessly, his icy eyes boring into the ashen-faced prisoner. 'What do you feel they would think of a common pervert like you, who sleeps with other men? Italians to boot? You think you could ever go back to Germany with that stain on your character, eh?' He paused momentarily. 'You know in your innermost self you couldn't. You are branded. There is no other way. Will you do it? Yes or no?'

Like a broken-hearted child the air-gunner began to sob, his head hanging down, mumbling something that was unintelligible to a horror-struck Otto. Docilely he let himself be led outside, shoulders heaving, while Otto watched, sick with self-disgust, and did nothing.

Five minutes later Kraemer and Todt were back, grinning broadly, the shifting corporal screwing his head to one side and giving strangled noises.

'Like clockwork!' was Kraemar's only comment. 'They'll find him in the morning.'

'Good,' Mueller said coldly and then his fat face lit up. 'Comrades that was his Christmas Present! Now for ours.' He looked around proudly at their expectant faces. 'We go out on New Year's Eve, Comrades!'

There was a triumphant cheer from the others, on their feet in an instant, faces aglow with excitement, clapping each other on the back happily. A sickened Otto slumped there unseen, recalling the air-gunner sobbing broken-heartedly that first night at the camp. Now he was hanging in the cold smelly latrine on Christmas Eve 1940. He could never work with this troop of blackguards again. He knew now that he must punish them, cost what it would.

CHAPTER 11

Somewhere a gate slammed back and forth in the howling wind. The snow peppered the windows of the huts like machine gun tracer-bullets. Everywhere in the deserted, dark compound the wind whirled the flakes into dancing, drunken snow-devils. Over on the other side of the wire, the Tommies were drunkenly singing their marching song, '*Roll out the Barrel*'. It was a perfect night for a breakout.

Now, one by one, the escapees stole from Pastor Mueller's hut and hissed through the whirling white gloom, perfectly camouflaged in the white woollen one-piece undergarment, and slipped into the Hole, with a triumphant Mueller patting each one on the back before he left and whispering, 'God be with you, my son.'

Now it was almost Otto's turn. Carefully he checked his equipment and supplies, the two tins of black market corned-beef, the packet of wet bread, toasted in the oven so that it would remain edible for a couple of days, the water-bottle of cold tea, laced with raisin wine.

Pastor Mueller smiled at him winningly.

'Don't worry, Otto,' he said, 'you won't be out long enough to have to worry about food. By morning we'll be in Hull and by nightfall I'll have found us a Swedish ship. Then we'll really eat – the Swedes like their bellies.'

'Yes *Herr Pfarrer*,' Otto said dutifully, keeping his head lowered so that the priest could not see the look in his eyes.

'*Ohne mich*,' he whispered under his breath and felt for the most important part of his kit, concealed in the inside pocket of his khaki tunic, which was now free of the blue patches that marked him as a POW – the home-made compass.

One of the Italians had made it for him in forty-eight hours at the cost of his whole month's cigarette ration, but Stahl knew without it he would be lost. The casing was made of a broken gramophone record, heated and moulded into form, with inside a piece of cardboard on which the points of the compass had been painted. A gramophone needle formed the pivot, and resting upon it, the direction needle – a bit of sewing needle, which had been charged by rubbing against a magnet. Otto thanked God he had learned how to use a compass in his years with the Hitler Youth back in Stralsund. He would need that knowledge tonight.

'All right, Otto, now you,' Pastor Mueller's voice broke into his thoughts.

'Yes, *Herr Pfarrer*,' Otto straightened up and edged the door open. The storm raged on.

'I'll bring up the rear, Otto, in five minutes. Off you go. God bless and protect you, my boy.'

'Hypocrite!' Otto said under his breath and then he was out, skirting the length of the wall like a white ghost, his feet almost soundless in the snow, the wind bringing snatches of the drunken Tommies song across to him, '*Now this is number one and he's got her on the run… Roll me over in the clover and do it agen…*' He frowned and prayed that the singing was only a cover, then he concentrated on the task on hand.

'They're all down below, *Herr Pfarrer.*' As the portly priest hushed into the door of the Hole, beating the snowflakes off his shoulders, Otto toiling at the pump, gave him the quick explanation. 'Digging the last of it out.'

At the entrance to the tunnel, Hans loomed into view and dumped another box of sand carelessly in the corridor. 'No need to worry about concealing it now, eh, *Herr Pfarrer,*' he said with uncharacteristic happiness.

'That's right, Hans. Tonight the *York Tunnelgesellschaft GmbH* goes into liquidation – for good. Ha, ha!'

Hans joined in the laughter and then disappeared from sight once again.

Down below they were digging upwards – a tricky, dangerous business. Already the previous night they had dug to within one metre of where they expected the surface to be on the outside and roofed the shaft firmly. Now Kraemer, the giant, was removing the soil on both sides below to make it big enough for them to exit and soon he would clear the roof support itself and start burrowing upwards that final metre, which separated them from freedom. If he did it too hastily, however, there could be a slide or cave-in which might block the tunnel for hours or a too massive hole might appear which could alert a sentry, even on a night like this. The digging-out was a difficult affair and even Mueller's usual bonhomie vanished now as the minutes passed by; the only sound – the howl of the wind outside and the steady gasping of the makeshift bellows as Otto pressed and pulled it at regular intervals. Over in their quarters, the drunken Tommies celebrating New Year's Eve were bellowing, '*Now this is number five and he's got her on the hive… roll me over, lay me down and do it again. Roll me over in the clover…*'

'Not only are the pigdogs obscene,' Mueller was saying, 'but they also have the audacity–'

'*Herr Pfarrer!*' Hans's urgent whisper cut into his words.

'Yes?'

'We're nearly there. Kraemer says there's only millimetres of earth separating him from the surface. He's waiting for your orders.'

Pastor Mueller breathed out a sigh of relief. Obviously the electric tension had almost been too much for him. '*Gott sei dank,*' he breathed out fervently, and lowering his head for a moment, his hands clasped in front of his portly stomach, which bulged obscenely from his white long johns, he sank into prayer, while the other two waited a little confused.

'Amen,' he whispered to himself, and then to Hans, 'All right, pass it on. We go out at midnight exactly. Not a minute too soon. They'll be drinking in New Year 1941. That'll keep the drunken sots occupied for at least fifteen minutes alone, the way I know those Tommies: beer-hounds.'

'*Klar, Herr Pfarrer,*' Hans snapped and disappeared below again to relay the message.

Mueller turned to Otto.

'I'm going down now, Otto, my boy. I hope my, er, girth will fit,' he flashed him a smile. Automatically Otto did the same. 'Would you be so kind as to stay pumping a little while longer? As I am sure you can understand, one needs a little fresh air when one's nose is pressed up close to Hans's, er, rear-end.'

'Yes, of course, *Herr Pfarrer*,' Otto agreed hastily, happy that the first stage of his plan was working without a hitch. 'He is a bit of an old fart-cannon, our Hans.'

Pastor Mueller disappeared and Otto prayed fervently he would never see that round, plump face with the faded blue eyes ever again.

The tension inside Adolf was electric. The escapers lay like cocoons in their white underwear, while at their head, Kraemer, his face sweating in the light of the little flickering candle, waited in excited anticipation. Behind him Todt kept craning his head round – as if he were attempting to hurry along the pastor to the rear – and dislodged a little shower of earth and pebbles each time he did so. Behind him Hans or someone was breathing in harsh shallow gasps like a dying man. Kraemer cursed yet once again and wished it would be midnight soon.

'Ten seconds,' Todt hissed behind him, passing the word along. 'Begin countdown!'

Trying to calm his racing heart, the big man started to count off the seconds, while to the rear of the line, Pastor Mueller did the same, his eyes fixed on the green glowing dial of his wristwatch, beads of sweat dropping from his forehead; in spite of the fact that Otto was still above, presumably pumping.

'Three… two… one… Midnight!'

'Midnight!' the joyous signal hissed from mouth to mouth up the line of sweating, tense men. '*Midnight!*'

'Midnight!' Todt barked sharply.

Kraemer needed no urging. He dowsed the candle immediately. Now they were in pitch-darkness, as he started to claw away at the remaining earth. The air became cooler. With difficulty the giant restrained himself. Gingerly, very gingerly, he picked the soil out with extreme care and then he felt no resistance whatsoever and knew he was through. Icy air and flurries of snowflakes were beating against his upturned face. He gasped for breath and commenced widening the hole, ears faintly picking up the drunken singing of '*Auld Lang Syne*' from the Tommies quarters. He grinned suddenly, in spite of his inner tension, as he remembered the English text. 'These particular old acquaintances'll be long gone soon, comrades,' he whispered to himself happily, reaching himself up... to receive the shock of his life.

They were well beyond the wire with its stork-legged towers, as planned, but only ten metres away, glimpsed clearly in spite of the whirling snow, there was a Tommy soldier – there was no mistaking those piss-pot helmets they wore – and he was staring alert straight in Kraemer's direction. He ducked his head.

'What the hell's going on?' Todt rapped angrily. 'Move it, you stupid Navy shit!'

The sentry heard the angry whisper immediately. He shouted something. A whistle shrilled alarmingly. A siren howled. There was the sound of motors starting up. Men were running abruptly everywhere.

'Go on, Kraemer!' Todt screamed fervently. 'Make a run for it now while there's still time!'

Kraemer swallowed hard and threw himself up and out of the hole.

'Halt, or... or I'll fire!' the unknown Tommy shouted through the howling gale.

But Kraemer was already running heavily for the cover

of a copse of trees some twenty metres away, followed by Todt, blundering crazily through the ankle-deep snow.

'Stop, or I'll shoot!' the Tommy cried a little uncertainly. 'I will! Promise!'

The two of them kept running, zig-zagging desperately. The sentry said 'Oh, Christ,' and pressed his trigger.

More by luck than good judgement, his first bullet struck the leading man. He staggered, his outstretched arms fanning the air like a seaside minstrel shaking his white-gloved hands at the end of his song, and then with dramatic suddenness he pitched face-forward into the snow and lay still.

'Jesus wept,' the sentry moaned, letting his rifle drop out of abruptly nerveless hands, 'I've shot him.'

'*Nicht schiessett Posten,*' Todt screamed frantically and came to a sudden halt, throwing up his hands in a paroxysm of fear. '*Bitte nicht schiessen!*'

And then he was standing there, starkly outlined in the harsh silver light of the searchlights which had flicked on the length of the wire, directing their beams outwards, the tears streaming down his thin shifty face. 'Bitte!... *Ich will nicht sterben!*'

The Tommy, shaking a little, raised his rifle a second time. But then a shadow raised itself up behind him, a shiv glinted in a crossing searchlight beam...

Otto tensed against the concrete support of the main gate, heart beating wildly, knowing that now he could be shot at any moment. The chaotic firing and the hard fingers of light probing the whirling white gloom – fortunately on the other side of the wire – told him that the Tommies were desperate.

This was good: his plan was working. But he didn't feel glad about it.

Renate, the dead air-gunner's 'little friend' had passed on the hint about the breakout to the right quarter. The Tommies had been waiting all right; the drunken singing had been a very good ruse indeed to lull the tunnellers into just the correct mood. The question now was – what were they going to do next?

Otto suddenly felt himself overcome with a wave of panic. The saliva dried up in his mouth. In spite of the freezing weather, he broke out in a cold sweat. His brain felt numb with fear. If some stupid sentry spotted him now, crouched down next to the gate, there could only be one outcome. Why didn't he turn and run like hell back to the safety of his hut before it was too late? There was still time.

No, a firm little voice inside him barked. *You're not going back Otto – not to that Nazi gang! You're going to get out of here, do you hear that? Out! Have courage… you're going to do it. Stick it out just a few moments more…* Just as that voice faded away, there was a roar of motors coming straight for the main gate. Harsh commands were barked nearby. The gate started to swing open. Dim blacked-out lights flashed momentarily, as the convoy of trucks sped into the camp. Otto knew what they were going to do. The men inside the metal steeds, white shrouded, helmeted figures with fixed bayonets, would attempt to seal off the other exit to the tunnel so that none of Pastor Mueller's men would escape. He pressed himself against the concrete post, praying that his long white underwear suit would camouflage him. It did. Running soldiers ran by him as if he wasn't even there.

Whistles shrilled. Men bellowed harsh orders. He could

hear Pastor Mueller's voice protesting angrily. 'But I am a Man of the Cloth, I tell you… a priest! I'll protest to the Swiss Red Cross about this… The King will hear–' There was a thud, a soft moan, and Pastor Mueller was heard no more.

In spite of his fear, Otto grinned. The fat bastard had taken one in the kisser at long last. The air-gunner had not died in vain. Next moment he was slipping by the one remaining sentry, obviously focussing on what was happening inside the camp, and running out into the whirling gale. The road to Hull was open.

Otto was free again.

CHAPTER 12

In years to come Otto would never understand how he made it across 'the Yorkshire Mountains', as he called them, that terrible snowbound New Year's Eve and morning. The nightmare trek that follows, left a lasting impression on Otto Stahl. Even today, shovelling down 'English-style paella' in that expatriate bar-restaurant on the Spanish coast and washing the muck down with a very un-English-style chilled champagne, a normally unsentimental, cynical old rogue like Otto could remember that night 'in the wilds of Yorkshire with every man's hand against me' very vividly: 'It was like that English book of theirs, *Withering Heights*, written by that Lesbian lady'. '*Wuthering*', I had been about to correct him, but then on second thoughts, withering did seem to describe the place better.

L.K.

At first the going across the flat plain that led eastwards from York was tough but possible. Using his compass the best he could, he followed the course of the winding road leading towards Hull, sticking to the fields, ploughing doggedly through the ankle-deep snow, head bent against the gale.

But after an hour of battling the snow, he gave up the fields and returned to the road, telling himself that nobody would be about on a night like this. But he was mistaken. In spite of the wartime shortages and terrible weather, the sturdy Yorkshire folk celebrated the New Year in one way or other.

He crept by a lonely farm-labourer's cottage. The regular squeaking of the bedsprings coining inside the tumbledown place indicated exactly how the humble farmworker was celebrating. Despite the freezing cold, Otto grinned and, wiping the snowflakes from his crimson face, whispered, '*Prost Neujahr!*'

From inside a woman cried as if in answer, 'Haven't yer come yet, Arthur? 'Cos its 1941 already, yer know!'

Otto disappeared into the night.

At three that morning, he was resting against a skeletal tree at the base of a great hill, preparing to ascend it by rubbing his weary calf muscles and clapping his arms around himself to keep warm. It was then that the sound of drunken singing startled him. A minute later a civilian came staggering down the hill out of the whirling storm, propelling his beer-filled belly in front of him, as a doting mother might push the pram containing her beloved first-born, singing, '*Show me the way to go home, I'm tired and I want to go to bed...* '

He saw Otto, standing petrified with fear against the tree. Politely, he tipped his cap, belched and said thickly, 'Loverley night for it, ain't it, chum?' He belched again and

Otto reeled back as the beer-laden breath struck him in the face, and then the drunk was gone, staggering off into the gloom.

At 4.30am he was creeping through the little town of Market Weighton. The British had removed all the place-name signs back in 1940 during the Invasion scare, but Otto had no difficulty in identifying the place. There were 'Market Weighton General Store', 'Market Weighton Post Office', 'Market Weighton Yorkshire Penny Savings Bank' all along the little main street.

Before him loomed yet another climb – *'like the Bavarian Alps it is in Yorkshire,' he cursed forty years later. 'You'd need to be a mountain goat to live there!'* – and again he paused to prepare himself for the climb, and again he realised that there were still people about. Opposite him there was a chink of light coming from a badly placed black-out curtain. Curiosity overcame his fear and he crept across to peer in.

He could only see part of the scene taking place within. The oil-lamp, the room's only means of illumination, kept flickering badly in a draught.

An elderly man stood there looking very serious, with what looked like forceps in his hands, while, next to him, a much younger fellow in a collarless striped shirt held a handkerchief to his eyes, as if he were crying, both their shadows wavering and magnified gigantically behind them on the rough wall. A baby was whimpering.

What the devil's going on, Otto asked himself. Had a child just been born? What was happening to the mother? Was there something seriously wrong? The looks on the two men's faces seemed to indicate that. Otto didn't know. He shook his head and struggled on, disappearing into the white whirling storm yet once again. In years to come, what had happened in that little house that night would always intrigue him. More than once he promised himself he would go back to Market Weighton and try to find out, but always the thought of those 'Yorkshire mountains' made him change his mind.

At six he was passing through Beverley. To his right the great Gothic Cathedral seemed to be sinking into the snow like some huge liner struck by an iceberg. Miserably he trailed through the deserted market square. A stray dog looked at him enquiringly, then it raised its shivering hind-leg and pissed contemptuously against the Fire Service's static water-tank. An exhausted Otto nodded.

'I know just how you feel,' he croaked in German.

Now he was only ten kilometres from Hull and he estimated he would reach the port before it became light. He forced himself to plod on.

'Four miles to Hull.' He had just made out the fading sign on a garage wall when he caught the first strains of a chorus of strong voices. He dodged behind a wrecked Triumph Super 7, lying there in the court, half submerged by snow.

A platoon of soldiers, swaying from side to side wildly, appeared out of the storm, kicking what looked like a beer-barrel in front of them, guided by a soldier who appeared to be wearing a pair of silk bloomers on his head and carrying a hissing carbide lantern in his hand.

'*Drunk last night, drunk the night before, gonna get drunk tonight like we never got drunk before. Cos we are the boys of the East Riding Yeomanry!*' They staggered by a crouched Otto singing wildly. '*Where was the engine-driver*

*when the boiler bust? They found his bollocks… and the same
to you. Bollocks…'*

With that derisive bellow they disappeared into the
storm once more and Otto came out of his cover, marvelling
yet once again at the stamina of the English. Give them
lukewarm beer enough, he told himself as he plodded on, and
they'll go to the end of the god-forsaken world. No wonder
they owned one third of the earth. They'd done it on
lukewarm beer.

One hour later he staggered into the entrance of an air-
raid shelter, built of brick, above ground and smelling strongly
of cat's pee, fish-and-chips and unwashed bodies. Tired as he
was, he scouted it out carefully. In the usual careless English
fashion, the door was not locked as it would have been in
Germany – something for which he was grateful. He crept
inside – and there stood a line of wooden bunks, without
mattresses of course, but such beautiful bunks lined with
planks all the same. His weary heart leapt with joy. With a
groan of delight he collapsed on the one in the furthest corner.
Exactly sixty seconds later, Otto was fast asleep in that
smelly, icy interior, snoring lightly. He was in Hull at last. His
nightmare journey was over.

Otto knew Swedes. As a boy, he had seen them often
enough in Stralsund, coming off the coastal freighters that
plied their trade between the Swedish Baltic ports and the
German one. He recalled them as mostly blond young men
with strangely unformed, somehow innocent faces (for sailors)
and no noses. They would step off their ships, head
immediately for the first store selling schnapps, and emerge
already guzzling the forbidden spirit straight from the bottle.

He'd heard that in their own northern homeland the stuff was severely rationed. They would set off looking for what appeared to be the second most important thing in their onshore life – women.

Now, sitting in that smelly Hull air-raid shelter, eating his bread and bully, washing the tasteless stuff down with tea, Otto planned his next step. Shivering a little with the cold, he reasoned he'd be most likely to come across Swedes where those two essential commodities were in abundance: easy booze and even easier women.

But how do I find such places, he asked himself. *That's the question.*

Three o'clock in the afternoon, 1st January 1941, Otto set off. The collar of his battle-dress was thrust up, his head was bent, and he slogged through the dreary red-brick streets of the port. He was following his well-trained nose, heading towards the water.

At first, as he trudged through the Yorkshire port city, heavy with the overpowering odour of stale fish, he thought the shabby civilians and the abundant servicemen, were watching him. But after a while, when no one stopped him and asked for his papers, he concluded they weren't. They were too concerned with having to face another year in this dreary place to be worried by strangers, however dishevelled and outlandish their appearance. Besides, he told himself, they had seen ragged seamen who looked as if they hadn't washed or shaved for all their lives.

Otto, he said to himself, *you're nothing novel here in this arsehole of the world.*

Around four he found himself in the centre of the port. Now the stink of fish and stagnant seawater combined made him want to vomit. He fought back the almost overwhelming desire and concentrated on his surroundings. He could see ladies of the night on all sides, standing in doorways, legs spread supposedly provocatively, whispering their professional endearments to passing males, stopping and pretending to fasten their garters when middle-aged Bobbies passed or poker-faced MPs, eyes like gimlets.

Naturally, servicemen were everywhere, viewing the whores, trying to make up their minds, egging each other on, fingering their shillings in their pockets, wondering if they could afford the prostitutes' services, perhaps scared that the 'women-of-the town' might give them something else besides a cheap thrill.

The sight of the young Englishmen parading up and down made Otto grin. They were much more timid than those German customers of his back in France. Boy, how he wanted to just lie on a beach in the sun, drinking Champagne right that moment. He looked around him. Instead, he was sniffing out Swedes on this shabby main street, which would be shattered out of existence, like so much of Hull, before this New Year was out.

But still, sex was what everyone was after.

'Sex fiends of the world unite', he whispered to himself in German and the whore he happened to be passing at that moment, called hoarsely from a doorway:

'I ain't got me teeth this afternoon, sailor boy... I could give yer a right treat for two and a tanner.' She grinned at him and clapped toothless gums together noiselessly.

Otto fled.

Looking back to make sure the old toothless one wasn't following, he wasn't focussing on where he was going.

Turning round again, he all but bumped into a lively group of young sailors, their Royal Navy caps set at a definitely non-regulation angle, laughing and talking loud. Skirting them quickly, he slowed to inspect them. *These guys might lead me straight to my destination*, he thought.

The lads were jaunty, ignoring the significant looks of the more sober civilians, telling them they shouldn't disturb the grey gloom of this grey coastal city. They knew they had a fifty-fifty chance of surviving the year. Otto thought of the devastatingly effective German submarine attacks he'd read about in the newly-created paper *Das Reich* back in France, the only article he'd looked at before throwing the thing away in disgust. His countrymen were sinking Royal Navy ships ten-a-penny, or whatever the English phrase was. If these young seamen wanted to be loud, they would be loud, and that was that.

On the spur of the moment, Otto decided to follow the young sailors. They were healthy, high-spirited and uninhibited. If anyone would find the Swedes for him, it would be the sailors.

The afternoon was spent heading from pub to pub the whole long length of Holderness Road which ran alongside the docks. At that time, the pubs were open illegally, charging prohibitive prices for the weak wartime beer. But the city's watch committee and the naval authorities turned a blind eye to this breach of the law. They knew they had to keep the sailors happy for their brief spell of shore-leave. Certain local Methodist preachers worked themselves into a frenzy in the 'chapels', fulminating against this 'devil's work' regularly. Every Sunday, in fact. Following the lads in-out-in-out, Otto knew none of this. He wasn't a student of peculiar English licensing laws.

Otto knew he needed a cover, difficult when his pockets weren't lined with English money. A little quick thinking later, he developed the simple expedient of picking up a half-empty glass of beer and carrying it with him from pub to pub. But after his third half-pint of the weak gassy stuff, he found the whole thing unnecessary. Everywhere in the crowded, smoke-filled places, full of the shrieks of brassy dyed blondes and the gruff curses and calls of sailors from half-a-dozen nations, drink was thrust upon him by perfect strangers.

After the sixth pint he found himself light-headed and wearing one of the sailors' caps, staggering along with them, being addressed as 'Dutchie' for some reason he couldn't recall, as if he had known them all his life.

It was in the *Ye Olde Black Boy* that his world started to whirl.

'The only good thing about Irishmen, is that a lot of them is dead,' someone was saying pedantically. A wizened Chinaman offered Otto a slice of rabbit pie and a glass of rum, whatever they were. Further down the bar, a Norwegian ate a razor-blade, his mouth full of splinters and blood. 'Irishwomen have got their legs the wrong way around,' the pedantic voice continued. 'What pox is sayin' tat?' came an Irish-accented reply. A sailor walked through a glass door to the 'gents' when it was closed, and didn't even pause when he smashed it to smithereens. An unassuming older lady took off her art-silk knickers and, crouching on top of a table, urinated into an ash-tray. The world whirled even more.

'The Irish'd sell their nippers to get at the poteen, the potato-faced bastards.'

'Whatever eejit's sayin' that shite about me homeland,

he'll end up arseways in the jacks!'

An old seaman with grizzled hair, took off his wooden leg in the urinal and sighed with relief. Otto was singing '*Roll out the Barrel*' in English, though up to that moment he hadn't known he knew the words.

A tart stabbed out her cigarette-end spitefully in the yellow of a fried egg, enjoying it, taking her time, her powdered face hard and set, as if she were burning out the eye of some hated rival.

'There's nothing that a good old dray-nag can do which your average paddy can do better,' the bitter pedantic voice persisted. 'They say there was once a Paddy who got so pissed, when he was on a pilgrimage to Rome that he kissed his missus – and beat old Pope Pius's foot to pulp.'

'Got yer, ye wee feckin' gobshite!' A massive Irish lad, built like a brick shithouse, picked up a short-arse with glasses and smashed his head through the plaster ceiling.

He sang *Deutschland über alles* and the sailors applauded, crying, 'First time we've heard the Dutch national anthem… sounds familiar!'

A woman with lips like a scarlet knife-flash across her white face gave him a feel under the table and said in a whisper, 'Bah gum, tha's carrying some weight about wi' yer. No wonder yer walking so bent-shouldered.'

The pub whirled and whirled and whirled. And then he saw him. There was no mistaking that strangely fluffy-faced sailor without a nose, drinking straight out of an upturned bottle of schnapps. He staggered wildly towards him, and threw his arms around his saviour.

'*Svenska… Svenska?*' he gasped.

'*Ja, ja… tak… tak,*' the Swede said calmly and took

another great swallow.

Otto passed out in his arms happily, clinging to him like a drowning man would to a life-belt. He had finally found his Swede.

CHAPTER 13

Otto groaned, moved his head, wished he hadn't, decided he was better off dead.

Anything was better than this Father, Mother and Holy Ghost of a headache that he had. It was as if red-hot skewers were boring slowly through the back of his head in the general direction of his eyeballs. His mind played repeats of Pastor Mueller's fiery speeches at a volume that wobbled his earlobes: 'We are but Mortal Men... Strayed from the Straight and Narrow Path... I hope my, er, girth will fit... Girth will fit... Girth will fit...'

But even through the blinding pain, he was becoming aware of a strange swaying motion and a kind of rusty, creaking sound. Was it the effect of all that English beer – 'ale' they called it? Perhaps it had rusted up his joints and every time he moved, he squeaked?

With an effort of naked willpower, he opened his left eyelid, moving it up over his red eyeball like an ancient, slow elevator. Now he could see! What could he see? Nothing. Just an expanse of dirty white wall. He decided he had passed out in the *Ye Olde Black Boy* urinal he had visited. He let the eyelid slip closed once more.

Time passed. Otto ached and ached.

The strange motion and squeaking sound continued.

Slowly it began to dawn on him that he couldn't be in a urinal. Piss comers didn't squeak, though they could appear to move to a drunk. Where in three devils' name could he be?

He considered the answer to that question at great length. For a dying man, he told himself, he seemed to be taking everything very calmly. Perhaps when one was about to die, one achieved a certain calmness of the soul. Yet –

Again he opened one eye. Now, in spite of what appeared to be a red-hot vice pressing together what was left of his drink-sodden brain with relentless inexorability, a room began to take shape in front of him.

The wall was not blank as he had thought at first. It was dotted at regular intervals with lines of rusty bolts, which seemed a little strange. Bricklayers did not normally put rivets in their walls. His blurred gaze moved carefully along the rivets. A faded portrait hung there, a cheaply coloured flyblown thing of a skinny-faced man in uniform. Vaguely it reminded him of the octogenarian King of Sweden.

He took his eye off it. Whoever it was, the man obviously didn't approve of him; he could see that from the look on the ancient wizened face. His search stopped abruptly. On a rack, there was a lumpy life jacket looking like a pair of stranded female bosoms. Just beyond it was a funny round window, splashed regularly with dirty green water, obviously by someone armed with a bucket outside.

Suddenly, horrified, Otto realised what the creaking and swaying was. He instantly knew where he was. 'Great bucket of shit, I'm in a *tank!*'

The door crashed open at that moment.

The 'Svenska' stood there, grinning drunkenly, a Royal Navy cap perched on the back of his shaven head, a tray balanced precariously in his big bony hand. Behind him, Otto caught a glimpse of a swaying green seascape.

'De whole gang is here!' he chortled in pidgin English and put the tray down at Otto's side. His twitching nostrils were assailed by the smell of fried fish. His stomach did a sudden back-flop. Now his headache was forgotten, but his guts were beginning to rebel violently. He forced himself to reply to the Swede.

'What gang?'

Svenska pulled out a half-bottle of whisky from his back pocket and took a tremendous swig.

'*Ja!* Everybody. De Navy boys... De Irishman... De hoors... de very busy now in de crew's quarters... oh, yes and de policemen from de docks.' He smiled, as if in fond recollection. 'Wat a party! Even de Kapitan got drunk and de first-mate had hard job finding the end of the estuary. Damn fine party, yessir. Dutchie!'

'You mean I'm on board a ship!?'

'*Ja, ja*, damn fine ship – Svenska ship!'

'But where are we going?' Otto blurted out.

'Where we go, Dutchie?' Svenska repeated a little stupidly and just caught himself from overbalancing as the ship swayed violently. 'We go Sweden... if we don't sink, ha, ha!'

'*Sweden*!'

'*Ja, ja,* Sweden. Funny ting. Dem dock boobies de was surprised as well when I told 'em. Want go over side. Over side in middle of North Sea! Ha ha!' He took another tremendous swig of the whisky. 'Now you eat fish.' He opened the cover and Otto turned pale. What looked like a small whale lay there in a sea of thick, burnt, rancid oil.

'Svenska fish. Good. Eat. Now I go and get Kapitan out of lav… Got stuck after party.' Then he was going, still drinking, of course.

Otto hastily clapped the cover down on the monstrous fish, as if it might be tempted to swim away, feeling his stomach heave and sway frighteningly.

'Ooooh,' he moaned in a contorted mixture of torture and rapture. His insides were ready to erupt at any moment. But even as he fought back that horrible feeling of nausea, his heart leapt with joy. He had done it. He had got away.

Then he was sick.

BOOK 2 – OUT OF THE BAG

CHAPTER 1

It was getting dark as the express from Kiel started to run into Hamburg. Already the lights twinkling across the broad silver expanse of the Alster, the port's inner lake, were beginning to click off one by one as the blackout curtains started to be drawn, and the anti-aircraft crews based along the banks were busying themselves with their searchlights, readying them for the Tommy bombers they had been expecting – in vain – since September 1939.

It was a moody Otto, dressed in the cheap blue suit the supercilious embassy third secretary had bought him in Stockholm, who stared out of the window at the elegant white-stucco villas that lined the lake. His initial euphoria at having escaped from England had vanished to be replaced by worry and bewilderment at his sudden change of circumstances. He was back in his homeland, that was true, but what could he expect here? What were the authorities going to do with him? He frowned, his mood seemingly echoed by the dismal clatter of the train's wheels over an iron bridge, as they now began to enter the inner city.

In Stockholm the day after the ship had somehow managed to dock – both the captain and the first mate were blind-drunk as usual, still running on the whisky bought by the case on Hull's black market – Svenska, the crew, the happy sailors, Otto and the bewildered boobies, as Svenska insisted on calling the two dock policemen, had one final terrific binge.

Next morning they had all shaken hands a little sadly, very hungover, croaking, 'See you after the war,' and such hopeless pieces of wit as, 'Give me regards to Mr Churchill,' and 'Tell old 'Itler not to bite any more holes in the Axminster, will yer,' and trailed off to their respective embassies to arrange some sort of passage home.

'This is gonna take a lot of ruddy explaining to the missus,' one of the policemen had grumbled, retrieving his helmet from the blonde girl who was wearing it and precious little else, and doing up his flies. 'By heck, and I bet she's still got me breakfast in t'oven!'

And that had been the last Otto had seen of his shipboard companions.

The officials at the German embassy in the Swedish capital had received him frigidly. The elegant young secretary in the dark jacket and striped pants had looked at him through his monocle as if he might well have crawled out of the panelled woodwork. He had stood there on the parquet floor, carefully avoiding the *Savonnerie* and *Aus-busson* rugs with his clumsy hobnailed English Army boots. Indeed, he had felt very much out of place in those surroundings.

Even the *Führer*, dressed in his simple brown uniform on the big portrait, seemed awkward, hanging there among the Watteaus and Fragonards on the walls.

'You say you actually escaped from an English prisoner-of-war camp, my man?' the foppish young official had exclaimed and then tittered discreetly behind the cover of his limp-wristed white hand, as if he were afraid of showing his teeth. 'How droll, how perfectly droll.'

'I'll perfectly droll you, you powdered-arsed pansy–' Otto had begun angrily, but already the young man in the striped pants had disappeared into some inner office, from which, in due course, came suppressed titters, as if he were relating the impossible tale to others of his kind.

He was interrogated for a full forty-eight hours by an old man who kept an unlit cigar in his mouth all the time he spoke, and wore a green ankle-length coat which creaked every time he moved, and had *Gestapo* written all over his leathery, old lecher's face. The ordeal had finished rather abruptly, and he was suddenly on his way back to Germany with a fourth-class rail ticket, a packet of liver-sausage sandwiches his only luggage.

Things had changed dramatically at Flensburg on the German-Danish border. While the train halted for custom and pass formalities (at that time the Third Reich still kept up the pretence that Occupied Denmark was an independent state), his wooden-benched compartment had been invaded by a group of excited Army officers and Party officials, led by the local *Kreisleiter*, an enormously fat man, who bulged out of his chocolate-brown uniform, the upper of his double chins resting on the immense roll of fat below like a head pillowed on a cushion. He had clicked to attention in front of an astonished Otto, bellowed '*Heil Hitler*' from a mouth filled with gold-teeth, and cried, 'And the *Führer* is right after all. England is no longer an island.'

While Otto had tried to comprehend that enigmatic statement, he had found his hand being pumped heartily and his back slapped by the whole jovial, noisy bunch, who herded him to a first-class compartment, obviously emptied hurriedly for his benefit, with a bottle of French champagne resting in an ice-bucket and selection of cold cuts and sausages set on the little table, the like of which Otto had not seen since that day he had been so rudely kidnapped from France the year before.

What does it all mean? he asked himself then, and it was the same question he was asking himself now, as the long express train began to draw into Hamburg's *Hauptbahnhof*, lit like a cavern in Hell in the darkening light.

With a final metallic clatter of its wheels, as if it wished to continue but was being forcibly restrained, the locomotive came to a halt. Otto stared out of the window and wondered what he should do. He knew no one in Hamburg, had five Reichmarks given to him by the embassy people, and was slightly befuddled on the French champagne. So while the other passengers fought their way out through the crowds of soldiers and civilians everywhere, he remained seated.

On all sides the enormous locomotives, painted with the slogan of the year, 'Wheels Must Roll for Victory', belched steam to the accompaniment of the loudspeakers blaring out military marches, interrupted at regular intervals by a flow of destinations.

'*Vienna, Paris, Warsaw, Rome...*' the very place names indicated the immensity of Hitler's new Empire, while the constant ebb and tide of troops symbolized the means of establishing that Empire and maintaining it.

From his window, he could see paratroops in their camouflaged smocks, black-uniformed tankmen, SS infantry with their death's-head badge and silver collar runes, elegant flyers from the Luftwaffe, men of the *Kriegsmarine* with their long beribboned caps: soldiers, sailors, airmen on all sides, who, together with the roar of the enormous locomotives, the blare of martial music, seemed to stand for the whole vulgar, powerful, vain world of the Third Reich. It was everything Otto had hated since his days at Stralsund. His mood of depression increased considerably. *What in hell's name am I going to do*, he asked himself.

His decision was made for him one moment later. Before his suddenly wide-open eyes, a red carpet was being rolled the length of the platform right up to the door of his compartment. Hurriedly he got to his feet. Outside a military band, steel helmets gleaming in the lights, was beginning to file up to the train. Obviously someone very important was still to get off. They were going to give a big 'civic welcome' to somebody. He better get out of the way quickly.

Clutching his cap, he reached for the door, opened it – and staggered to an abrupt stop as if he had just run into a brick wall.

Immediately to his front at the other end of the length of red carpet, there was a small group of high Party officials and officers, heavy with medals, ornamental daggers, swords, and swastika armbands. To the right of the carpet there was a battery of microphones, to its left a crew of cameramen and press photographers, with, extending out in a line on both sides, shivering bare-kneed boys and girls in Hitler Youth uniform, holding little swastika flags at the ready.

'Holy Strawsack!' Otto gasped in sudden panic. 'I'm in the *Führer*'s way!'

Wildly he looked to left and right for a means of escape, but officials were beaming at him to his left *and* right. He started wondering where those black-uniformed thugs were. He'd seen them accompanying Hitler back in Holland when he'd received his Iron Cross Second Class. Perhaps it was Goering they were expecting, all lipstick and rouge, his chest weighed down with innumerable medals; or even the club-footed Doctor Goebbels, surrounded by his female star mistresses, always a head taller than he was; even the gloomy miserable Hess peering out from beneath his thick bushy eyebrows like a bewildered, lost savage from some patch of primeval jungle.

And then a shiver passed over him. Maybe it was the dastardly Himmler, head of the SS – the man who wanted Otto's head on a platter for defiling that idiot Dirk van Dongeren's mistress. If Himmler was anywhere to be seen, Otto would be in for it! Out of one prison and straight into another.

But no, there was no one else here except – Otto did not complete the thought.

The immensely tall drum-major had raised his baton high, as if he were about to brain somebody with it. He brought it down sharply. The brass band clashed into a thunderous rendition of '*Heil Dir im Siegeskranz!*' sending the pigeons flying up to the glass roof in protest.

The officers saluted. The Party officials thundered '*Heil Hitler!*' and at the back of the waving children, a distinguished-looking middle-aged man took off his English-style bowler for some reason or other.

Otto stumbled forward onto the carpet, mesmerized. This reception... Everyone here... They were all looking straight at *him*. But why?

A hard-faced man with clever eyes stepped forward and seized Otto's hand.

'Kaufmann... *Gauleiter*... Hamburg...' He barked out

the words like bullets from a machine-gun suffering from a bad stoppage. 'Welcome... Hero...' He lowered his voice suddenly and spoke very rapidly, as if he didn't want the others to hear. 'Smile at the camera, look pale but heroic. The old poison-dwarf,' he meant Goebbels, the Minister of Propaganda, 'likes modest, pallid heroes.' And with a quick wink, 'There'll be a very good French girl waiting for you at the hotel. I can personally vouch for *her*.' He raised his voice again and continued in that staccato style of his, while Otto stared at him in complete bewilderment. Pallid heroes... girl in the hotel... What did it all mean?

'Now,' Kaufmann was assaulting the assembled crowds, 'the perfidious English... know... their island... is no longer impregnable! Here... is the living proof... The first escapee... from their dreaded... concentration camps! The first of *many*, folk-comrades!' He frowned meaningfully, thrusting out his heavy jaw dramatically, as the cameras whirred and clicked and the flash-bulbs popped. 'I promise... you... *that*.' He thrust out his hand and pumped Otto's. 'Otto Stahl... welcome to Hamburg!' He beamed hugely at the bewildered young man, who blinked anew every time a flash-bulb exploded.

It all hit Otto in a flash. He was a national hero! He groaned inwardly. Now he really was back in the Third Reich.

A few minutes later the welcoming ceremony was over and to the accompaniment of the *Badenweiler*, the *Führer*'s own favourite march, he allowed himself to be guided to the *Gauleiter's* own big black Mercedes like a dumb animal being led to the slaughter. The children waved as they walked into the night. The officials and officers hurried after them to the exit, and behind them on the platform, the gentleman in the

English-style bowler frowned down with thoughtful contemplation at his impeccably rolled umbrella. It was unused, even though it had been raining hard in the wet northern port of Hamburg. Then, finally, he too departed into the night.

CHAPTER 2

The French beauty *Gauleiter* Kaufmann had promised him had come and gone. She had stayed all night. Now he was alone again in the deluxe second-floor suite of *Hotel Vier Jahreszeiten*, overlooking the Alster, shaving himself happily in the mirror.

'Come and gone!' he said to himself, scraping carefully down one side of his handsome face. 'She's gone and I've come!' He laughed at his own humour. But there was something to it, he told himself.

The girl, a fragile blonde with a black parting, had been very business-like indeed, referring to herself as a 'working prostitute who was forced to like the hard men of the Reich', as she had unzipped her skirt without any encouragement from an overwhelmed and, by this time, slightly tipsy Otto (Kaufmann had kept him at the hotel's magnificent bar for over an hour, introducing him as 'Our Hero' to the local worthies and newspapermen who promised to splash his story over the headlines the next day).

After she had called him Anna twice at a moment of real or supposed ecstasy, he realised that she probably didn't like any hard men at all. All the same, after months of enforced celibacy it had been good, very good. Even the dreary raindrops running down the huge windows of his suite like sad tears could not dampen his good mood this particularly wet morning. Otto whistled '*There'll Always be an England*' and concentrated on his chin.

A little while later, just as he was patting it dry, there was a soft knock on the door. Thinking it would be the waiter, who had promised him breakfast 'with real bean coffee', Otto called, 'Come in.' And then, 'Put it down on the table, waiter,' as he continued to dry himself. 'I'll get to it in a minute.'

'Put what down, Herr Stahl?' a woman's voice queried. Otto spun round and dropped his towel hastily to cover his naked loins.

A young woman and a pretty child were standing there, the child staring at him with the kind of intensity one might expect from a little girl faced with a tall, naked man, trying to hold a small face towel over what was left of his dignity.

'What... who...?' Otto gasped.

'Just your autograph, Herr Stahl,' the young woman said sweetly. 'For my little girl, you know. She's making a collection of heroes. We've already got Herr Kapitan Lieutenant Priem'.

'Priem... a hero?' Otto stuttered. 'What's going on?'

Triumphantly, the woman held a copy of the local Hamburg paper to reveal the glaring headline complete with his photograph taken the night before.

> *HERO OF POW CAMP BREAKOUT.*
> *Otto Stahl first German POW to escape*
> *from English Concentration Camp.* Führer
> *sends congratulations.*

'I knew we'd be first, Herr Stahl,' she said proudly.

'We took the workman's special from Bergedorf. Didn't even have breakfast.'

Otto forced a smile.

'I see,' he said a little helplessly, though he didn't. 'Your... er... book?'

'Book!' the woman rapped to the bemused child. Open-mouthed, still staring unabashedly at the tall naked man, the child produced the book, and the mother said, 'Have you a pen Herr Stahl? We've forgotten ours.'

Otto gulped. It seemed the stupidest question he had ever heard. With considerable fumbling, manoeuvring his towel like a badly trained striptease dancer, he moved across the room to the antique writing desk, where there was a pen. With all the dexterity he could manage he signed the child's autograph book, while the young mother beamed at him before saying, 'Now give the uncle your hand, darling, because he has been so kind.'

'Oh balls,' Otto groaned and holding on to his towel with one hand proffered the child the other one.

'Thank you very much,' the mother said. Leaning forward, both hands clapped to the little girl's ears so that she couldn't hear the final words, she hissed. 'What manhood you have, Herr Stahl... Any time you fancy some relaxation... telephone-book under Kroeger, Eli.' She winked knowingly. '*He* works nights.'

'Of course,' Otto said weakly as the door closed behind her. He collapsed on the bed.

All that morning, Otto kept being disturbed by hushed-voice civilians who wished to shake his hand, wanted him to relate the details of his 'tremendous escape from the perfidious

English', give them his autograph, or simply just touch him wordlessly, as if the mere contact, like in the case of kings of old, would solve all petty problems.

That damp morning, while anonymous well-wishers from below kept sending up bottle after bottle of German champagne, he placed his name on everything and anything from hotel menus, through identity cards, to human forearms – 'Sorry, Herr Stahl, but I forgot to bring any paper.'

Twice young women of the town invited him home for 'Coffee… and things'. Once a young lance-corporal in the Luftwaffe with marcelled hair and smelling of *eau-de-cologne* made a somewhat similar offer, though not quite.

Two hours later, Otto was heartily sick of being a hero.

At about 11.30am when he was staring moodily at yet another bottle of champagne sent up from the bar by yet another 'admiring well-wisher', his phone rang.

Marshalling his wits about him, he picked up the receiver. It was the front desk, he told himself, forwarding yet another starstruck Hamburger.

'Not another bloody fan?' he almost shouted into the thing.

'I'm afraid not,' replied a very polite voice. 'Just a little business, if you could be so kind?'

The call came from Goebbels's Ministry of Propaganda in Berlin. The official apologized for disturbing him, and took Otto's apparently off-hand reply to his question at its face value. But it was a worried Otto that replaced the receiver. He knew instinctively that his days as a hero might be short-numbered. The polite official had asked what particular branch of the service had he belonged to before he had been captured by the English. He had vaguely replied, 'the infantry', but he knew this wouldn't keep German officials happy for long.

Soon they would be enquiring the number of his battalion and that's when the trouble would start. How could he get away with explaining that a young, highly fit man, as he was, had been running a mobile brothel in France instead of serving 'Folk, Fatherland and *Führer*'?

Some fifteen minutes after the disturbing enquiry, the phone rang again. Otto picked it up hesitantly. Was it perhaps the Ministry again, asking for more disturbing details that would ultimately end up putting him in prison?

But the voice that greeted him at the other end was fruity, full of aristocratic confidence – and very well-remembered.

'Otto, my boy! *Meadow* here. Just in time. I need your help. The car will be waiting for you at the side entrance to the hotel in ten minutes' time. Check if you're being followed or anything, would you? Splendid. Till then!'

'What?' Otto stuttered. 'Car... Followed? By whom?'

But the phone had already gone dead in his hand, leaving him to stare at it, as if it had just produced a kind of small miracle – a voice from the dead!

'Good morning, sir,' the tall chauffeur said politely, raising his uniform cap and with his other hand opening the door of the gleaming Horch limousine for a bewildered Otto to enter. 'Rather a nasty one, I'm afraid.'

'Yes, rather,' Otto stuttered, too puzzled even to ask their destination.

The chauffeur got into his seat and picked up the speaking tube. 'If there is anything you wish to eat or drink, sir,' he said in that too refined voice typical of an upper-class servant, 'you will find it in the box at your feet. I should imagine you would care for a little music, sir. Radio Hamburg is broadcasting a Furtwangler concert this lunchtime.' Without waiting for Otto's reply, he clicked on the radio and thus launched them into near-midday traffic to the accompaniment of Furtwangler conducting the *Führer*'s favourite work of Wagner, '*Tannhauser*'.

Twice, Otto tried to find some means of opening the glass partition between him and the high-class chauffeur and ask him just where they were going, but twice he failed. Concluding that it was locked, and unable to find the speaking tube at his end, he took a bottle of beer from the box and drank slowly as they sped across the Lombard Bridge, along the Esplanade, past the Bismarck memorial, by Dammtor station discharging its thousands of passengers like maggots out of a large green cheese, and then picking up even more speed into a newer district of the great port.

The shabby, red-brick nineteenth century houses disappeared to be replaced by modern white-stucco frontages, set back in large gardens, which Otto judged might well have been built in the 1920s. It was obvious that they were expensive, and the bemused young man in the back of the big Horch thought that if 'Meadow' lived out here, he was doing very well for himself once more. A lot seemed to have happened in half a year!

Five minutes later the chauffeur turned off from the Elbchaussee into a secluded, yet wealthy-looking side-street. He changed down and guided the big car carefully into a tight drive, the gravel crunching under the tyres in that impressive fashion of prosperous and quality entrances. He stopped, got out, and repeated the same dignified performance he had given at the *Hotel Vier Jahreszeiten*.

Almost as if he had been hiding behind the curtains waiting for this exact moment, a portly figure in the striped jacket, white gloves and bow tie of the German butler appeared, umbrella at the ready, calling, 'Please don't move, sir… I'm coming!'

Trying to remain dignified and at the same time prevent Otto getting wet, the fat man did a strange sort of quick shuffle towards the bewildered guest, not allowing himself the liberty of protecting his own balding pate with the umbrella from the raindrops, until he had Otto firmly covered by it. Together, they moved to the house.

'The master is waiting for you in the study, sir,' he announced, as if Otto frequented the big house every day and knew both who the 'master' was and the location of the 'study'. Gently, he guided Otto round till he was facing an open door. The smoke of an expensive cigar drifted out into the hallway, as did strains of the same Wagner concert the chauffeur had decided he should hear in the car. The portly butler patted off the last drops of rain from his shoulders like a loving mother preparing a son to meet his new headmaster for the first time. In a daze Otto started to walk through the doorway, but was immediately pulled back by the portly gent, who, getting in front of Otto, announced, 'The Hero of England, Escapist Extraordinaire, Celebrity of the Morning Paper, Herr Otto Stahl!'

A tweed-clad figure, smoking a cigar, was seated in front of a roaring fire, a glass of what looked like whisky standing next to him on a little table. At the man's feet, on a great white furry rug that looked as if it must have come from

135

the biggest polar bear there had ever been, a red Irish setter reclined, tongue hanging out like a piece of red leather. In the background, Wagner smashed on ruthlessly in brass-bound Teutonic fury.

The figure didn't move, seemingly transfixed by the music. Otto hesitated and then cleared his throat.

The seated figure still didn't move. The smoke rose slowly from the expensive cigar, the dog continued to pant as on the other end of the radio, Furtwangler whipped his sweating musicians up to a frenzied climax.

Otto cleared his throat again, a look of slight desperation on his face now. 'Excuse me, but–'

Suddenly the tweed-clad figure sprang to his feet and rushed towards him with surprising speed.

'Otto, my boy!' that familiar upper-class voice exclaimed joyfully.

'Meadow – I mean, Count. It's you!' Otto cried and then they were in each other's arms, slapping one another on the back, babbling away excitedly like two silly schoolboys, while in the background Furtwangler's musicians slammed the Wagnerian discords from one side of Hamburg Radio's studio to the other with absolute, complete abandon.

CHAPTER 3

Otto stared at his old friend, whisky glass in one hand, big expensive cigar like a small flagpole in the other. He still couldn't believe it.

They had sat down either side of the fireplace. Graf von der Weide, whose old *Abwehr* code-name had been 'Meadow,' smiled back at him from the other chair, as if willing him to open his mouth and start asking the questions that were whirling through his head at that moment.

The Count looked ten years younger. Gone were his priest robes of their beachfront kerfuffle. The fat had also gone and now his face was lean and adorned by a trim grey moustache so that with the tweeds he was wearing, one could have taken him for a retired English officer, or perhaps a senior officer in civilian clothes. Everything around him seemed to fit into that particular framework, too. The dog, the roaring, open fire, a rarity in Hamburg, the whisky, even the cigars. Otto noted that they certainly weren't the cheap German products. Otto would not have been surprised if the Count had opened his mouth and begun speaking to him in English.

Instead, the Count reached over and patted his knee affectionately, saying in German, (though somehow his new clipped intonation sounded slightly English), 'Bet you were surprised to hear from me again, you young hero, *what?*'

'That is the understatement of the year, Count,' Otto said, taking a gulp of his whisky, while the dog snored softly at his feet. 'But... how...?' Still the question he wanted to ask refused to formulate itself correctly in his jumbled brain.

'All in good time,' the Count said gently. 'But first of all, I'd just like to hear something on Radio Hamburg.' He flashed a glance at his expensive gold wristwatch. 'It'll be on in a minute.'

'The radio?'

The Count held his hand up for instant silence. Somehow or other, Otto told himself, he had regained his old confidence that had vanished during his enforced leave of absence from the *Abwehr*.

The warning gong sounded. It was one o'clock.

'*Hello, Germany calling... Germany calling*,' a harsh nasal voice snarled in English, a voice which though Otto did not know it then, was to become the best-known, after Churchill's, for years to come in England – and also the most-hated. The voice continued in English:

'*Let me tell you, my listeners, the good news first. The Pope in Rome has launched yet another peace offensive with the full support of the* Führer *and the German Reich. Germany is satisfied with her victories. But what of Churchill, I ask you. Does he want peace? Can a bloated plutocrat like that who turned his guns on the workers back in 1926 tolerate–*'

Otto let the words, only half of which he understood, run on, staring in bewildered at the entranced Count, yet oddly impressed too by that harsh, bitter cynical voice.

Finally, the studio gong sounded again and the bitter venomous propaganda broadcast to England, full of boasts, threats and cruel jokes about the 'corruption in the British ruling-class', ended. The Count rose to his feet and switched off the radio, saying, 'The treacherous swine, though I suppose one ought to be grateful for small mercies.'

'Treacherous swine?' Otto echoed, completely perplexed now. 'But he's working for Germany.'

The Count ignored the comment. 'Do you know what they call that swine in England?' he asked.

Otto shook his head.

'Lord Haw-Haw. People in the know say that he gets as many listeners when he broadcasts that vile rubbish as does our beloved Mr Churchill.'

'Beloved?'

At last the Count seemed to become aware of his guest's bewilderment. 'Look,' he said, 'let's refill our glasses, Otto, before I start. It's going to be a long story, and I need you bang up-to-date.'

'Start – start what?'

'The account of how I came to join the British cause,' the Count said with some dignity. 'A warrior for Mr Churchill!'

'Holy strawsack!' Otto exclaimed. 'You'd better get another bottle, Count!'

'It was a strange journey, through the night from Dover.'

Otto nodded his understanding and settled back in the deep leather armchair, as the Count set about the account account of his mysterious business in England.

'Hour after hour of journey, until finally that nice young officer who did the interrogation there at Dover – something like Captain Smith-Wanking, one of those double barrel names – helped me out of the car and I found myself in a remote country house, no sound save that of the sentries pacing the grounds. Very fine lawn they had, by the way.'

Otto sniffed. 'Officers obviously have a different kind of war from us common blokes.'

The Count did not appear to hear. 'But the occupants weren't asleep, no, not one little bit,' He wagged his finger at his handsome blond listener. 'The English are a very alert and cunning people, perfidious Albion and all that.'

Otto thought of the sentries who fell asleep over their Bren guns at York, the drunken singing the night of his escape, but he said nothing; he was too intrigued by the story the Count was telling.

'At first there were two of them there, obviously gentlemen out of the top drawer. One could see that immediately. The one was a dried-up fellow with thinning hair and devilishly clever eyes. Between you and me, I know now that he was the head of their Secret Service. They call him "C". The letter stands for the English word "cunning".'

'How cunning?'

The Count did not react. 'The other was clearly a military fellow in mufti. Also very smart though a little more direct than this Cunning chap. Kept getting up from his chair all the time and swinging a golf club all over the place as if the study were some tremendous links course or something. Spoke German, too. Well, at least, he said hello in German when I was escorted in by Wanking-Smith or Smith-Wanking or whatever he was called.'

(What the Count didn't know, and Otto only found out years later was that the

*military man was a certain Col. Mason-
MacFarland, the pre-war military attaché
to Berlin, who had just been relieved of
his post as head of the British
Expeditionary Forces' Intelligence
Service. The other was, of course,
General Stewart Menzies, head of MI6. –
L.K.)*

'So all this swinging happened in the middle of the night?' Otto asked slowly.

'Yes, I suppose you're right, my boy. Perhaps Mufti's German wasn't so good after all. But one thing is for certain, he knew his Germany and he knew all about me,' he lowered his voice dramatically. 'Everything.'

'Damn!' Otto breathed, impressed.

'Damn indeed, Otto. He knew all about my activities with the *Abwehr*, Old Father Christmas's plan to – er – dispense with the *Führer* in May 1940 and my particular role in that unfortunate affair. The whole bloody lot.' He nodded significantly.

'Then the other one, this Cunning chap, said: "Count, we know that you are a good German, one with his heart in the right place, one of us in other words." The man was obviously some well-born aristocrat, Otto, I could see that at a glance. One of us.'

'Naturally,' Otto said sarcastically, 'a typical aristocrat like me – father unknown and mother earning her pennies on her back in bed.'

'You are one of *nature's* aristocrats, Otto. I have always told you that, but pray let me continue. After this Cunning had finished singing my praises, he came out with the reason for having me brought there.'

Otto leaned forward eagerly and his face was warmed by the fire. 'Yes?'

'He said he'd like me to meet a third party, who was waiting for me in the other room.' The Count could hardly restrain his excitement now. There was almost a feverish glitter in his eyes. 'A very important person indeed, he emphasized that, fixing me with a look like a cobra about to strike some petrified animal prey.'

'Who was it, Count? Come on, spit it out! Not King George himself?'

'No,' the Count smiled triumphantly. 'Someone far more important than he.'

'Pee or get off the pot already!'

'Don't be so plebeian Otto,' the Count teased.

'Who?'

'A certain Colonel Warden.'

'Colonel Warden?' Otto's face fell. 'And who's *Colonel Warden* when he's at home?' he demanded, his honest young complexion reflecting his disappointment.

Instead of answering his question straight out, the Count teased his young listener a little while longer, while the logs crackled merrily and the setter continued to snore, occasionally giving out little pants, as if he were enjoying some erotic doggy dream. 'A moment later Colonel Warden came into the room in person, exactly as I had always imagined him, though a little smaller than I had anticipated, with a lot of cigar ash on the lapels of his jacket. I had always thought he was a very tidy person somehow.'

'Who?'

The Count feigned not to hear. 'Of course, it was the middle of the night and he had been imbibing slightly. Not serious, of course, but I did think without the stick he might well have keeled over a couple of times.'

'Who?… Who was it, in God's Name?' Otto cried out in exasperation.

'We, of course, rose and then this Cunning chap did the introductions, but naturally, as clever as he was, he couldn't fool me. That cigar and whisky glass were sufficient. Even if they had covered his face, they would not have been able to fool me.' He, winked knowingly. 'I would have recognised who Colonel Warden really was anywhere and anyhow.'

'HEAVEN, ARSE AND CLOUDBURST!' Otto roared, springing to his feet, 'WHO WAS THIS COLONEL WARDEN SHIT?'

Graf von der Weide looked up at his infuriated, red-faced young friend with a mild grin on his face. 'I thought you would have guessed by now, Otto. I'm surprised at you. Colonel Warden was – of course – no less a person than their prime minister, Winston S. Churchill!'

CHAPTER 4

'I'll have another double, Stew,' were the Great Man's first words as he slumped down hard into the chair. 'Little soda, if you please.'

C rose obligingly and mixed the scotch, while the Count and the Englishman with mufti and golf club stared down at the rosy-faced, cherub-like politician in his 'siren suit', a one-piece garment that made him look like a rather fat, bald-headed baby.

Churchill indicated that they should sit and for the first time turned his gaze on the German. In spite of the drink and the lateness of the hour, Graf von der Weide could see the keenness in those eyes and knew instinctively he was in the presence of greatness; it was the same feeling he had experienced the day Hitler had presented him with his Iron Cross. He realised they were both very much like one another, the *Führer* and Mister Winston Churchill.

'Are you by chance a father, Count?' he asked unexpectedly, his words slurred a little by his badly fitting false teeth and perhaps also due somewhat to the whisky.

'I don't think so. Perhaps. I have never married,' he stuttered, bewildered by the question.

The confused answer seemed, however, to satisfy the Great Man. He took a reflective sip of his scotch and said, 'It is good that you have not, my friend,' he growled. 'Ordinary men should have children naturally – for the sake of the nation's future. Even less ordinary ones should, perhaps – for the sake of stock.' He raised his finger in warning, as if he were addressing a full session of the House of Commons. 'Great men should refrain!'

The Count flashed an enquiring look at his two other companions, but they remained silent, offering no explanation of what the Great Man meant, so he ventured a hesitant, 'How do you mean, *Herr Ch–*' he caught himself just in time – '*Herr Oberst Warden*.'

'*Herr Oberst Warden?*' Churchill rolled the words across his tongue in an atrocious accent, but with obvious pleasure, 'I like the sound of that. German is a fine language for cursing in, I always think. *Herr Oberst Warden*. Yes. I don't think I have been addressed with a German military rank since '04 when I accompanied the Kaiser on the Imperial manoeuvres of the year.' He smiled suddenly. 'And I doubt if your Herr Hitler will ever honour me with a German military title, what?'

There were polite titters from the ether two Englishmen. Churchill's plump cherubic face grew grim again.

'Children, Count,' he declared, 'compromise great men. They never live up to their fathers' greatness. When I think of my own brood…' He sighed and continued. 'But what if the great man is indiscreet too, and if he sires a child on the wrong side of the blanket, if I may put it like that?' Suddenly he straightened up from his slouched position in the big leather armchair and declaimed grandly:

'*There have been, or I am much deceived, cuckolds ere now. And many a man there is, even at this present, now, while I speak this, holds his wife by the arm. That type that thinks she has been sluiced in his absence. And his pond fished by his next neighbour, by Sir Smile, his neighbour...'*

'Yes,' the Count said, feeling more confused than ever.

'That was from "*The Winter's Tale*",' Churchill said as much to himself as the assembled gentlemen.

What was all this about, the Count wondered. Where was Churchill leading him with all the talk of children and lechery? He felt himself growing red: he had never been comfortable with such talk very much.

Churchill dipped the end of his cigar in the whisky and sucked on it thoughtfully for a moment, while in the background the old grandfather clock ticked away life in heavy metallic solemnity. He surveyed the Count's fleshly face, as if he were considering whether he should continue or not. Apparently he came to the conclusion that he should do so, for as the sentry's boots started to crunch by on the gravel outside this remote country house.

He leaned forward and said, 'Great men – and this might come as a surprise to you – also have their vices.'

'Not really a surprise, *Herr Oberst*. I know from personal contact that the *Führer* likes cream cakes, though to the outside world he represents himself as one who disdains such things.'

Churchill laughed. 'I do not mean the pleasures of the stomach, but of the bed, my dear man. Your Frederick the Great and his young men, Kemal Ataturk with his child mistresses of both sexes. Napoleon, who I believe thought the tongue was more important than the other thing.'

The Count flushed even deeper and the one called Cunning looked at his highly polished shoes. MacFarland got up and started swinging his golf club at imaginary balls, watching them sail away through the sash window into the night.

Churchill was amused by their reactions.

'When I was a young man,' he continued, 'starting my political career at Bath – a surprising place to do so, come to think of it – I attracted the interest of a comely young woman, who was already married. She had some vague interest in politics in the fashion of better-educated women at that time, though thank God, she never fought for female suffrage. When I think of all that chaining themselves to the railings and throwing themselves under the King's horse and then elect as their first MP Nancy Astor... Ah well, but that's another story.

'Now then, Count. To make the business as short as possible. A delightful little encounter between the sheets and once in the rather cramped back-seat of my campaign car; there was an unfortunate mistake – The Honourable Reggie Gore-Browne!' Churchill sighed, as if he were a sorely tried man.

'Kicked out of Harrow, my *own school*. Buggery! Sent down from Balliol. Indecent exposure! Sacked from the Foreign Office. Importuning in Hyde Park! Quietly banished to Switzerland to learn languages. It was thought there would be nothing in that dull little country to tempt him. But we didn't know our Honourable Reggie Gore-Browne well enough yet, it seemed. Deported two days after he arrived. Gross indecency! Something to do with another like-minded soul in a public place on a Sunday afternoon. I think the fact that it was Sunday afternoon upset those staid Calvinists more than anything else.

148

'Thus my blow-by-blow arrives in *la belle France*, where blessed with ample money by his doting mama and unsuspecting pa, he spends his time between Paris's springtime debauchery and Cannes with its winter vice. For ten whole years that was the kind of life this young rogue pursued. He devoted himself completely to his unnatural vice, never once lifting a finger to do a stroke of honest work. Indeed, my dear Count, the only decent thing he has ever done in his whole worthless life is not to make public that I am his father. That secret is known to a very limited, *select* group of people. Up to now!'

There was a sudden note of bitterness in the Great Man's voice. He took a timid sip of his drink before saying, 'You tell him, Stew, I am a little overcome.'

The Count's heart went out to the stricken figure slumped in the armchair opposite him, deep lines abruptly etched in his plump face.

'Yes sir,' the man they called Cunning answered promptly. 'Well, you see, Count... *Oberst Warden's* son was in Paris when the German Army marched on in this last summer and he was immediately apprehended as an enemy civilian.' He frowned. 'Needless to say he had not volunteered for the colours in'39 as any decent young Englishman would have. In spite of his little – hm – peculiarities, the Guards would have granted him a commission, especially the Coldstream.'

'Among his other defects,' Churchill said without looking up, 'Gore-Browne is first and foremost a devout coward.'

'In the camp just outside Paris where the Germans placed him, he came into contact with a group of renegade

Englishmen who, I regret to say, were preparing to actively collaborate with the enemy.'

The Count tut-tutted, then realised abruptly that he was that 'enemy' in question. He stopped immediately.

'There was no fight, I trust?' he asked.

Cunning smiled, though those cold eyes of his did not light up. 'That would not be Gore-Browne's style, Herr Graf, nor those who were with him in Paris. Too dangerous. People get killed fighting, you see. No, these chappies wanted to fight with pen and paper – and their tongues.'

For a moment the Great Man's strange remark about Napoleon flashed through the Count's mind and he reddened again, until Cunning explained what he had meant.

'They offered themselves to the Germans as volunteers for their propaganda machine.'

'Goebbels' Ministry?'

'Exactly, Count. To write his lies in his English for him and broadcast his untruths over the wireless.'

'A sorry bunch,' Churchill raised his head and took up the explanation once more. 'Fools, dupes and more than a few rogues like Gore-Browne. A bunch of our local breed of fascist – thank God we bagged Mosley in time – and of course, *my scion!* Now, I have long given up caring a fig about what he does, though it does hurt me to find my son among such rabble. But what, my dear Count, if he knows he can gain further advantage with the Germans by disclosing one really great secret to Goebbels's propaganda minions?'

'That you are his father, I presume.'

'Exactly.'

'You realise, Count,' the one with the golf club said urgently, as if he were afraid that the Great Man might reveal his true identity, '*Oberst Warden* is a very important man in this country. A scandal of that kind could have serious political consequences. God knows what the Americans would say. They are a very moral people and their Ambassador Kennedy thinks we're finished already, at least that's what he tells President Roosevelt.'

'It would shake the conservative back-benchers at the very least,' the Great Man said with a bitter laugh.

'Now, we know,' MacFarland continued, 'that these wretches are being led or trained or what have you, by a certain William Joyce, known locally as Lord Haw-Haw. He was one of Mosley's pre-war fascists, a renegade who went to Germany just before the war broke out.

'He is brilliant in his way, a real rabble-rouser, and there are unfortunately a lot of nice Nellies in this country who believe him rather than the good old BBC. Naturally, like all such people he is an empire-builder. He wants to shine in the German eyes with the number of people, especially important ones, he can convert to the German cause. He is training them, so we understand, to become a serious thorn in our side. We have received intelligence, too, that Joyce has decided to take our little rabble to Germany, either to the Berlin or Hamburg region, where they have their transmitters for broadcasts to England.' He broke off suddenly and looked at the Prime Minister and then at the man called Cunning, as if he were afraid to say any more.

For a few moments there was a heavy silence, broken only by the metallic ticking and the faint hush of the wind in the skeletal oaks outside.

Finally Churchill spoke. 'Herr Graf, we would like to make you an offer.'

'An offer?' The Count's mouth was dry with excitement. After all those laborious weeks spent at the helm of a travelling circus, he was now being thrust right back into the thick of it. *Finally,* he thought to himself, *excitement and adventure!*

'Yes. We want to offer you your freedom, unlimited funds supplied through a friendly agency operating out of the US Embassy in Berlin, and, erm... Oh, blast it...'

'The holiday house,' C murmured to his shoes, prompting the Great Man.

'Yes, yes, I've remembered it now,' he retorted. 'And when everything is over, Count, a rather nice villa on the Greek coast. If you wish, of course. Otherwise I'm happy to keep it,' he added in a hurry.

The Count, overwhelmed with joy at the prospect of adventure, stuttered, 'But what would I have to do, sir?'

'Find Gore-Browne. Take him from the place where he is presently located, to Athens where our people will ensure that he becomes a permanent remittance man in some South American banana republic. And he can stay there for good, indulging in as much buggery as the local authorities will allow, but where he will worry us no more, sir.'

'But what if he would rather stay in the Reich?' the Count objected, his mind racing wildly at the news. Freedom, money, and above all, excitement once more.

'Then, sir,' Churchill said slowly but firmly, 'you have my permission to... kill... my son. In whatever way you please.'

CHAPTER 5

There was a long silence after the Count had finished his account of that strange midnight meeting with the English prime minister. The logs crackled and on the white steppe of a rug, the red setter twitched in dreamy doggy ecstasy. Otto sat dazed. What had impressed him more than anything else, was that the Count had reproduced all the accents. *He must have worked on them for hours.*

Finally Otto said, 'You accepted?' He couldn't help let a note of incredulity seep into his voice.

'I am here now, aren't I,' the Count replied modestly. He stretched out his well-cared-for hands, as if to embrace all the luxury about him. 'The Horsemen of Saint George bought all this. The car, the chauffeur, the butler too, my boy.'

'The Horsemen of Saint George?'

'Yes. Gold sovereigns. They have been riding for the English these many centuries now and believe you me, Otto, they are always victorious. Money usually is.'

'But you could have taken the money and run, Count,' Otto protested. 'Don't you realise just how dangerous all this is? The *Gestapo*... The–' he stuttered to a stop. Obviously the Count didn't.

'Otto, I may not appear to be a very realistic person to you. I know you have been forced to have a great deal of patience with my – er, strange little ways at times. But I do attempt to keep my ear to the ground.'

'And what does your ear tell you?' Otto asked sarcastically, but as always sarcasm was wasted on the Count.

'That before this year is out, America will be in the war on England's side, and with the United States helping her, England will win. Sooner or later the Hitler regime will fall and after what I have been told of the hidden brutalities of the Reich by my London compatriots, it will be a good thing indeed.' He lowered his voice. 'Do you know they are making soap out of Jews in the camps?'

Otto groaned. 'Have you just found out, Count? They've been slaughtering Germans too ever since 1933. Big strapping fellers, dying all of a sudden of heart attacks and the flu once they were inside the camps. But then they were only working-class blokes and nobody worries much about them, do they?'

The Count looked a little thoughtful. 'Yes, I suppose you're right.' Then he brightened up again. 'But what do you think, Otto, my boy? Are you with me in this new adventure? Once we've helped our Mr Churchill to get rid of the evil Nazis, it'll mean a medal for you. One you can keep, this time! You'll be a genuine hero. Unlike your present predicament. After all we are dealing with the top people in London and they know how to look after their servants, I can assure you that, *what!*' It looked like the Count was Anglicising his accent to fit his new-found character.

'I'm a hero right now,' Otto replied a little sourly, 'and I can tell you it's ruddy tiring. I'm glad it's only temporary! Finally, Count, I must remind you that it always seems when we little folk deal with the top people, as you call them, that we always end up soaked through and hung out to dry.'

The Count frowned. 'In a way I suppose you're right. The Great Men always seem to land on their feet. Must be some sort of law of nature.'

'Yeah, the devil always shits on the biggest heap!' swore Otto, frustrated now.

'Now don't turn bitter and cynical on me, Otto. I always have been concerned *greatly* with your welfare, remember? And I am concerned for you now.'

'What do you mean?'

'You are a hero today, but what of tomorrow, my boy? Our authorities are, as you know, of a somewhat suspicious and pedantic nature. Sooner or later they'll find out about you and your desertion from the *Abwehr* and all the rest of it. What do you think will happen then, *what?*'

Otto remembered the official call to his hotel room that morning and knew that the Count was right. They'd find out soon, and what then? He hardly thought it possible that they would jail a hero, but at the best, he'd find himself in uniform. He'd end up fighting for that monster in Berlin whom he had sworn, back in August 1939, he would never serve.

The Count sensed his young friend's resistance was weakening. He continued urgently, 'It is a tremendous challenge, an adventure, with *great* rewards at the end of it. Imagine, Otto, on a cold damp day like this, a villa on the Aegean! The sun, the wine,' he hesitated momentarily, 'the girls.' He blushed. 'Away from it all in a nice warm neutral country, sitting out the war until our Mr Churchill has won.'

'Our Mr Churchill, oh shit!' Otto mimicked the Count, then said resignedly, 'All right, I'm with you. Now tell me, what's the situation?'

LEO KESSLER

'Marvellous! My dear chap!' The Count bounded forward out of his chair to shake Otto's hand. On the rug the setter gave a contented sigh, and wagged its tail before settling down to a peaceful slumber. 'I can't do it without you. You see, I need your dashing good looks.' Before Otto could question that, the Count dashed on. 'My man will serve lunch at two, Otto, if that is not too late for you? Good. I think I could fill you in with the details before then, eh?'

Otto couldn't help but laugh at his friend's boundless energy. 'Fire away!'

'This Gore-Browne chap and the rest are being kept in a small country house out in the Sachsenwald near Bismarck's estate at Friedrichsruh. It is a suitably remote rural location and as far as I have been able to gather. It is well guarded by the local police and, naturally, by those SS dogs.'

'Naturally.'

'They are regarded as guests of the German government – these blasted renegades – but after all they are English and everybody knows the English are a little peculiar at the best of times. They're not to be trusted. Therefore this Joyce chap, who's in charge and now technically a German, is taking no chances. To all intents and purposes Schloss Farthheim – that's the name of the place – is hermetically sealed off.'

Otto absorbed the information. 'And what are these funny Tommies supposed to be doing there?'

'Herr Joyce, this Lord Haw-Haw traitor, is supposedly training them in their future activities for the Poison-Dwarf Goebbels, writing scripts, preparing news bulletins and that sort of thing. The word is that Goebbels has given him unlimited funds because the *Führer* wants to talk the English into surrendering rather than being forced to take military action against them. He has other plans.'

'What plans?'

'That I don't know, Otto, but there is something in the air. I can smell it. There are large troop movements taking place every day now and Germany itself, or at least this part of it, is being denuded of aircraft in spite of the danger of British bombing.'

Otto thought of all the troops he had seen at Hamburg *Hauptbahnhof* the evening he had arrived at the port, and told himself the Count could be right.

'And your plan, or the lack of it?' he joked.

The Count beamed at him. 'It is *all* planned, Otto. Money opens many doors. A rather large contribution to our dear Roman Catholic Church has obtained for me a special pass. I fear the dear Monseigneur who sold it thought I needed it to shirk my duty as a loyal German and not join the forces, but the Church of Rome, despite what some people think, is a broad-minded organisation, especially if the Vatican's coffers are filled.'

'Come on then. Out with it, Count!' Otto said, chivvying his friend along. 'How you gonna get into this Schloss Farthheim place?

The Count reached down and produced a familiar sort of shovel-type old-fashioned black hat. Otto groaned inwardly.

'As Father Flynn,' he said, placing it on his head delicately, 'the Pope's own special representative from Rome – of course I'm an Irish neutral – to see and report on the lot of these unfortunate Englishmen incarcerated there.'

Otto was laughing openly now, as the Count arranged the hat on his head and flounced around the room in it. 'Father

Flynn indeed! Some Irishman you'll make!'

The Count turned back and looked him in the eye. 'I speak the language, you know... *Begorrah!*'

Not more than twenty kilometres away from that house where the Count revealed his plans to a disbelieving Otto, another Irishman, a real one this time, was detailing some of his own to a mixed crowd of bored young and middle-aged Englishmen in the dark panelled hall of Schloss Farthheim, already derisively nicknamed, 'the Fart Home'.

William Joyce, once of London's Jewish East End during his days with Mosley's fascists, spread his legs apart, thrust his thumbs in his belt, a look of absolute contempt on his razor-scarred face, and rasped in that incisive nasal voice of his, 'Gentlemen, may I have your attention?' He looked around at his 'scribblers' as he called them privately, in their leather-capped tweed jackets and unpressed grey slacks, and added, 'If you are to serve the fascist cause, you must observe fascist discipline.'

'Oh, put a sock in it, old chap,' someone called out from the crowded hall.

Joyce ignored the comment. It was typical of that kind of upper-class Englishman, whose ranks he had once attempted to join, without success.

'All of you have some talent or ability, due to your training or background. Of your own free will, without any coercion on the part of the German authorities, you have decided to place it at the disposal of the Third Reich. Good. And you may rest assured that one day our own beloved country will benefit from that ability, for it will ensure that England will enjoy the benefits of the fascist creed.'

Reggie Gore-Browne let out a jaw-aching yawn. He was a medium-sized man in his thirties, with a round unwrinkled face, balding sandy-haired head, cynical eyes heavy with old lecheries and an alertness, always ready to see in every new male contact a potential partner. From the third row, he gazed at Lord Haw-Haw. Old Joyce was laying it on thick again.

Who cared about Germany, England, or even the British Empire? It had always been there and would probably go on, long after Hitler, Joyce, his father and he were dead. It was all very tiresome.

He had thought that when he had volunteered to help them out with this silly little war of theirs, he might meet a better class of man. He was sick of sailors; greasy-haired youths who carried tins of Vaseline with them and were all too obvious; pimply, bespectacled hesitant clerks, all red-faced, clumsy and 'what will you think of me?' and hairy-armed butchers, who could only think in terms of rape and humiliation.

He had thought, back in Paris, he might meet a more artistic sort of person, with a bit of soul, who had been to the right sort of school and knew people 'in town'; a kind of Somerset Maugham type. He had been disappointed.

They were all hall-baked intellectuals of one kind or another, who couldn't even get the old John Thomas up, or lithe suburban fascists, who were terribly shocked and puritanical when one made an approach. He yawned again. It was all so frightfully, utterly boring, he couldn't help blinking.

'Once I defended the British Empire. I was proud of it,' Joyce was snarling. 'All that red on the map. One third of the world. Now, what is it? It is like the Modier Country: shabby, antiquated, bankrupt, rapidly running down like an old clockwork toy engine.' He sucked in a deep breath, while Gore-Browne's bored gaze turned to stare at Schmitz of the SS.

'Now the only hope for the old country is innovation, an influx of German blood.'

Gore-Browne sucked his teeth.

'I wouldn't mind a little influx of German blood,' he remarked to himself, taking in Schmitz's handsome figure in the smart black uniform. The youth had white-blond hair, candid blue eyes and a tall, intelligent forehead. He looked like a figure one might expect to meet in the *Nibelungenlied*, a perfect advertisement for the Germanic creed Hitler was propagating. Yet at the same time there was soul in there too, Gore-Browne decided. He was ever the closet romantic.

He could well imagine himself, at this very moment, having delightful little chats about 'love' and such things with him – afterwards; and there was no denying the man was virile. There'd be no trouble about the old John Thomas with him! It would all be like Isherwood and that wonderfully decadent Berlin of the pre-Nazi era, he thought. He sucked his lips and pinched his cheeks to give them some colour, beaming winningly at the SS-man.

Schmitz blushed and looked away.

Aha, that's significant, Gore-Browne told himself. *He is one of us.* They all were, whatever their protestations about their masculinity and their perverted pretence of skirt-chasing.

Joyce was coming to the end of his regular harangue and from experience Gore-Browne knew he would be expected to contribute a lot of propaganda bullshit to the following discussion. He dismissed Schmitz from his mind for the moment. But in his heart he knew that the gorgeous German was worth a small sin. But what exactly was that sin going to be?

CHAPTER 6

'Schloss Farthheim!' the Count proclaimed, as he parted the dripping bushes and the building resting on the height to their front was revealed to Otto.

The weather was bad again. The drizzle came down with grey and miserable persistence. But Otto, who had walked here down cobbled country lanes typical of Schleswig-Holstein, had been glad of the rain. It had kept the local policemen in their village offices, or more likely in the village alehouses.

They had left the big black Horch behind the Bismarck Museum on the outskirts of Friedrichsruh, the big estate granted to the man who had created the new Germany single-handedly, by a grateful nation of the previous century.

'He shouldn't have bothered,' Otto had grunted when Count had told him the story.

'Sometimes, Otto, I think you're right,' the Count had commented, taking his eyes off Bismarck's wax dummy inside the single-storey red-brick building – he looked like a great sad-eyed walrus, wearing a spiked helmet. 'Perhaps the world would be a better place without a united Germany.'

Now they were moving in for 'a spot of light reconnaissance', as the Count had put it. Both of them were dressed in old clothes, their backs covered by wet potato sacks so that any curious policeman might take them for local farm-labourers returning home after a hard day in the fields. At least that was the Count's plan, though Otto wondered how long he would fool anyone who had eyes in their head. It wasn't every farm labourer who wore a monogrammed gold signet ring on his well-manicured hand and smelled delicately of expensive after-shave instead of manure. *No matter*, he told himself. *Now we're here, we might as well get on with it.*

Cautiously the two of them crept closer to the castle on the height, all mock Gothic battlements and intricate, complicated nineteenth century architecture, bent under their sacks like hunch-backed monks.

On the far side of the place there were lime trees and chestnuts, branches flying in the wind. Thinking back to his hey day of breaking and entering, Otto noted the place, telling himself that it was hidden from sight of the guards in their little red-and-white striped sentry boxes at either side of the castle entrance. He followed the Count into a copse of wet trees. This was close enough for their observations, for now they could hear snatches of a song coming from somewhere in the dilapidated battlements, patched with clumps of turf and green fern.

'I say,' the Count said indignantly, 'it's "*There'll Always Be an England*," the feller has the impertinence to be singing. That from a *traitor*, Otto. It really is too much, *what!*' Then his anger vanished as they settled down to study the place and he said, 'Some Intelligence fellows out of the Berlin's US embassy gave me a run-down of what's what. That castle wing on the right is the canteen, in the centre is the hall used for lectures, and the wing on the left, overgrown with creeper, houses the dormitories.'

'Well, if we can get out of the dormitory windows, it's only a short sprint to that set of limes and chestnuts, Count. Look.'

'Brilliant, Otto. If everything goes tits-up we'll squeeze our way out of a barred window, fall a whole ten metres and race for the trees on our broken legs. You're here for your good looks, young man, not for your brain power.'

Otto, who had always thought he was rather well-endowed with intelligence, was quietly affronted. But then, next to the Count, his intellect was probably insignificant.

'I wonder what it's like in there, Otto, eh?' the count mused. He'd obviously moved on.

'I could tell you, Count,' Otto said a little grimly, remembering his own imprisonment in York, 'but I won't. You're too delicate. All I'll say is this. Inside places like that, you'd become even more crazy.'

Reggie Gore-Browne lay on his bunk, arms under his head, staring gloomily at the flaking ceiling and listening idly to the chatter all around him.

Tea had been a thin peppermint brew, two slices of black bread, smeared with candle grease and ersatz plum jam, and was now finished. Instruction was over and they had a whole night to kill until Herr Joyce made his next appearance at nine o'clock the following morning. It would be, Gore-Browne told himself miserably, a long, long night.

'My man refused to leave Paris and join me,' the elderly queen, who had once run a *gentleman only* salon in the French capital, was saying in an affected falsetto. 'The perfume I've used for years is absolutely unobtainable even on the black market and my friend, you know him Pierre, that divinely handsome apache-type – "Pepe le Moko", I used to call him – has gone off with some Boche colonel. I really do think the war is spoiling everything, Algy.'

'If we are not entitled to a bit of respect,' the middle-aged freelance journalist, who affected a hacking jacket and a pipe, was grunting through puffs, 'what are we fighting this war for? I mean I have the greatest respect for Herr Joyce, but he isn't a real journalist, is he? People like me, who have worked for the *Trib* and have done a stint with the *Times*, don't like to be told how to use an exclamation mark!'

Gore-Browne groaned inwardly and closed his eyes. Sleep was now his only solace – and the dreams it brought. Even when he couldn't sleep properly, he would close his eyes and suspend himself in a protracted semi-sleep for hours on end, knowing that when he opened them again, the prison-like atmosphere would come crowding in again with its bitchiness, stupid-important chat, its posturing and overwhelmingly boring routine. Why, he asked himself once more, had he ever been fool enough to volunteer for this sort of thing? If only he had a lover!

He thought of the handsome SS officer Schmitz and licked suddenly dry lips, as if in anticipation. He could imagine if he told that repulsive product of the Irish bogs, Joyce, who his father really was, they would take him away from this dreadful place. All doors would be opened for him.

By now he thought he knew the Germans. They ran on about 'unnatural vice' and all that, but they were as corrupt as the next country. He had seen the covert looks Schmitz had thrown at him when he thought that he, Gore-Browne, wasn't looking. He could imagine that the authorities, once they realised his real value, would close a blind eye to anything he could manage to pull off with Schmitz. 'Pull off' – the phrase triggered a delightful image. Schmitz stripped of that handsome black uniform, completely naked. How white and delicate his body would be! Gore-Browne groaned. Suddenly he burned with desire.

A half kilometre away, a wet, miserable Otto shivered in his sacking.

'Count, my eggs are rapidly getting hard-boiled in this bloody cold. I've seen enough. Let's get back to the car and you can tell me how we're loot the Bastille where it's warm!' He shook his head in mock self-disgust. 'Just got out of one freezing cold prison, and now I'm catching pneumonia trying to break into another! What a crazy world.'

The Count grinned and agreed. 'I've got a flask in the car, Otto. That should warm you up.'

'I'll need a shitting blow-torch to thaw my feet out.'

Fifteen minutes later they reached the Horch, wet and weary. No one had seen them. The whole of Schleswig-Holstein seemed to be disappearing behind curtains of thick grey rain. Otto, dripping with water, threw down his soaked potato sack and blew a raspberry at the waxwork Bismarck. 'Schleswig-Holstein, Bismarck, you can have it! I'd give it back to the Danes. They've got webbed feet!' And with that he slipped inside the front of the Horch.

The motor spluttered into life, and the Count turned the heater up full-blast. As the warmth began to flood the front, he handed Otto his silver flask of cognac, and began to speak. 'I must admit I have not worked out the plan to the final detail. A certain amount of, ah, improvising will be necessary.' He grinned winningly at Otto.

Over the top of the flask, the other man gazed fixedly through the windscreen.

'Ah, yes,' backtracked the Count, 'Well, I think, however, on the whole, it is a very tidy little plan. We won't have any trouble getting in. The pass is genuine. Hitler wants to appease the Pope Pius and the Catholic Church. There are a lot of German Catholics, I mean, who like that sort of Papist thing.'

'Oh yeah, and then,' Otto asked gruffly, feeling better after a few sips of cognac. In front of him Bismarck's walrus face was beginning to disappear rapidly, as the windscreen steamed up in the heat. That was something to be thankful for at least.

'Our problem is really GB,' this was their new codename for Gore-Browne. 'I see it as a twofold one. First, to convince him he should come with us. Second, how to get him out of the camp when he has made the decision to come with us.'

Otto nodded his agreement, but said nothing. Bismarck vanished completely. He took another drink of the cognac. It burnt right down to his toes.

'Phase two, I feel we can manage relatively easily,' the Count continued. 'The Horch has a remarkably large boot. It's also comfortable. I asked my new butler to try it out on his job interview, you know. I told him he was a great fit for the role, and signed him on the spot! Ha ha, *what?*' Getting no response from Otto, he collected himself and continued. 'I doubt, too, that the guards will be tempted to search the boot on our way *out*, especially after we have distributed wine from it – blessed by His Holiness the Pope himself – to the sentries on our way *in*.' He looked slyly sideways. Maybe this would be cunning enough to elicit a response from the young fellow.

'You're a crafty old devil at times,' Otto was forced to admit, a little happier now. 'But how about phase one? How are you going to convince Churchill the Queer to come with us? That sort of warm brother tends to like such places. I know from experience! and I don't see you, Count, gunning him down if he doesn't want oblige.'

The Count shuddered dramatically. 'Please don't say things like that, Otto.' He winked at his handsome companion. 'Have you never thought, my dear boy, that you are a very attractive chappy?' he said slowly. 'You'd make a rather fetching chauffeur, I would imagine. Uniform, in spite of your dislike of it, suits you very well.'

It dawned on Otto what the Count was hinting at. 'Oh, my aching arse,' he groaned. 'Not that!'

The Count looked at him sternly. 'Now Otto, we don't need to go that far,' he said piously. Then he grinned. 'But you've got the right idea.'

Hunched over his cognac, Otto continued to stare through the misted-up windscreen. This had been the Count's plan all along. Hadn't he said something about Otto's good looks at their reunion meeting? *This is why he needed me and not just one of his British cronies*, he thought to himself. *He's probably read up on Gore-Browne's previous boyfriends and realised I was just the type.*

'When are we going in?' he asked in a small voice, and then winced at his own turn of phrase.

'Tomorrow afternoon,' the Count replied, and taking hold of the gear-lever. 'Now I think we'd better get off home, my little jewel in the rough. It's going to be a long day tomorrow, and you need to be looking dashing!' He pressed the button activating the Horch's windscreen wipers. They flicked back and forth. Bismarck came into view once more, staring at them with his bulging, bellicose eyes. Otto blew him another raspberry and then they were gone.

And up in the castle, lying on the bed in his own turreted quarters, *Hauptsturmbannführer* Schmitz was reading Bismarck's memoirs (for after all, he was on holy ground). His eyes took in the lines of text. '*He who has just administered a thrashing, will undoubtedly receive one the next time round,*' and shuddered delightedly, the phrase recalling beautiful memories of those years at Eton.

He dropped the thick tome and forgot Bismarck's warning to the victors of the 1870 campaign against France, his mind full of those thin supple canes. How beautifully they had hissed through the air when wielded by one of those ascetic-looking perverts in their black gowns. He had always fantasised about being tortured by some cowled monk of the Inquisition, in spite of the exquisite pain on his naked boyish rump.

Although the English regarded themselves as mild-mannered, polite, easy-going people, they were, in reality, he knew, an arrogant, aggressive lot with all the hard-handed, cruel roughness of a very wealthy nation.

Cold-blooded as they were, they only *talked* a great deal about fornication, but did very little about it. In Schmitz's mind, most of their women were either lesbian or flat-chested creatures, who didn't believe in 'that sort of thing', anyway. In short, he had realised very quickly arriving at Eton that he had come to his spiritual home. The sense of deep guilt that it was very un-Germanic even to think such things, slowly became pushed far back into his brain. How absolutely delightful those beatings had been! How his heart had jumped with joy when one of the housemasters had produced his cane from up the chimney! And how wonderful those cold-blooded fornications in the cubicles later!

'Ah,' *Hauptsturmbannführer* Schmitz sighed in English, Bismarck and Final Victory completely forgotten now, 'those were great days!'

He thought of the plump Englishman with the balding head who had looked at him so knowingly the other day – Gore-Browne he was called. Joyce had mentioned him before. He looked the type who might just use the cane. He shivered with delighted anticipation and told himself that he would venture to speak with him on the morrow. The new war campaigns would soon start and time was running out for him. Yes, tomorrow it would have to be.

Hastily the handsome young SS officer turned out the light, thrust the cane (he had had them sent specially from England before the war) in between his teeth and imagined he was being bound and gagged by some black-gowned, perverted sadist in the way he always did. Within minutes he was groaning and rolling with wild pleasure. In that tremendous exploding moment of culmination, he cried out loud, '...for Eton!'

CHAPTER 7

'Turn out the guard! Officer approaching,' the black-clad sentry at the entrance to the castle barked smartly, the raindrops glistening on his black-painted helmet.

Behind the wheel of the big Horch, flying the flag of the Vatican proudly at its gleaming bonnet, Otto, dressed in the chauffeur's uniform, started to slow down. The guard tumbled out of the wooden hut and lined up. Behind him 'Father Flynn' took his eyes off his breviary and straightened up, as befitted the official representative of Pope Pius.

At a snail's pace, they approached the line of black-clad sentries. The drummer rattled his kettle drum, and their hard hands slapped their rifles, running through the routine of the salute, each gesture trained and perfect. Their heads moved woodenly with the car as it slid to a stop. *Their heads are worked by steel springs*, thought Otto, staring out of the windscreen as fixedly as he had done the previous day.

Benignly, Father Flynn turned in the back and blessed them with an affected movement of his right hand.

The Guard Commander strode up and saluted with the customary '*Heil Hitler!*' barked at them as if they were standing five hundred metres away and not five.

Father Flynn blessed him too and then brought out his papers. Formalities were over in a matter of moments and

Father Flynn indicated to his smart young chauffeur that he should open the door of the big boot. Otto did so and then the Papal Representative insisted on giving each man a bottle of wine 'blessed by the dear Pope himself' and shaking his hand, which proved a little awkward, as each man was standing rigidly to attention. Five minutes later they were driving under the castle portcullis, leaving each sentry with a bottle of wine placed at his feet, like a line of urine samples at a military medical.

Well that's the first part over, Otto told himself with a sigh of relief. They were in! Now the questions was – would they be able to get out?

'I was at Eton,' *Hauptsturmbannführer* Schmitz commenced a little awkwardly, as he fell into step with Gore-Browne. It was the midday break and the cobbled castle yard was full of Englishmen taking the air after a morning of lectures.

'Were you really?' Gore-Browne feigned enthusiasm, delighted that the handsome young SS officer had finally spoken to him, though a little disappointed that he was an old-Etonian. They were renowned for not having 'souls' at Eton.

'I was kicked out of Harrow!' he said, fluttering his sandy eyelashes in what he imagined was a modestly seductive manner.

Now it was Schmitz's turn to be kittenish. 'Flogging your fags too severely, I expect?' he said in a small voice.

'Something like that,' Gore-Browne agreed.

'With canes!' Schmitz breathed. 'Sp… spanking them too hard!' he said the secret word with his heart fluttering excitedly.

'Yes, I suppose,' Gore-Browne said, a little puzzled,

but with his blood rising anyway.

Schmitz sighed with relief. 'There is nothing like the strict corporal discipline of a public school, I always think.'

Gore-Browne said nothing. He was slightly bewildered by the trend the conversation was taking, but the gorgeous German was talking to him, that was the main thing. Now they were heading in the direction of the castle's wing that contained Schmitz's room. *Can it be on purpose?*

Trying to control his excited breathing, he said, 'At Harrow, they didn't use the cane on the grubby little fags. Mostly the beater found a cricket bat made more of an impression.'

'I say!' Schmitz was obviously impressed. He thrust his own arm through Gore-Browne's, as if they had known each other for years. 'My dear chap, this is really interesting. You must please tell me more. Cricket bats... '

'Lift up yer hearts, my boys... God bless, lads... *Begorrah*,' the Count passed through the yard, raising his black-clad arms like crow's wings at regular intervals, blessing the puzzled Englishmen who stood around, with their hands in their pockets, viewing his efforts with a mixture of bewilderment and amusement. 'Shape your lives to the gravity of the hour, *begad*. God bless...'

The Count went on remorselessly, his eyes darting here, there and everywhere, searching for GB, occasionally flashing a quick glance at the photograph of him which C had supplied back in London, hidden within the pages of his pocket bible.

Up in his turret room, William Joyce followed the absurd progress of the tall priest with burning, contemptuous eyes. He had just added the old trick of noting that the clock had stopped at some public place – this time outside St Pancras Station – to his script for the evening broadcast. It made his listeners believe that Lord Haw-Haw was omnipresent with his spies everywhere. Of course he didn't know whether St Pancras's clock had stopped or not, but the ruse usually worked; English clocks seemed notoriously unreliable. Now, indulging in a tea break, he watched the man from upon high.

What fools the Germans were, he told himself, as the Papist flapped from group to group looking like a bloody black crow, so like the English. Why did they permit all this *petit-bourgeois* nonsense with the Red Cross and parcels from home and all the rest of it? Were they not always maintaining that they were as tough as leather, as hard as Krupp steel? In practice, they were soft. Hitler had no real conception of the fascist ethic, hard, brutal and intolerant. He snorted with poorly suppressed anger. One day the *Führer* would learn.

Then a sudden flash of inspiration sent his tea cup clashing back into his saucer. He forgot the absurd priest and returned to his evening broadcast. '*Now where is your vaunted Ark Royal?*' he scribbled quickly. '*I shall tell you. At the bottom of the sea, to be precise, sixty fathoms deep in the Mediterranean,*' He sniffed and told himself that this was the third time he had sunk the aircraft carrier this last six months. He hoped this time that High Command had got it right at last.

Otto was relishing his role. All through his body, nerves were tingling with electric tension. He had never felt less bored, than right now, playing the part of the bored chauffeur. He was just thinking how alive he was feeling, when he spotted GB. The 1939 passport photo of the target had been clear, and he recognised the man immediately.

'But, damn it, what's this?' Otto cursed to himself.

There was an awkward catch. GB was in deep conversation with an officer of the SS! And to top it off, they were strolling arm-in-arm across the cobbled courtyard towards the ivy-covered dormitory wing of the castle. Otto hesitated only a fraction of a second. 'Father Flynn,' he called.

The Count swung round. 'Yes, my son,' was his mild reply. Then he saw the look in Otto's eyes, followed the nodding of his head and caught sight of the two figures strolling towards an ivy-framed doorway. Reacting very quickly, he disengaged himself from the gaggle Englishmen.

'Take the car over there, my son,' he ordered. 'I would like to distribute the last of the wine to the people in that building.'

'Yes, Father.' Otto prevented himself from running to the Horch. He swung himself into the driving seat, started, and crawled in first gear across the courtyard. Passing GB and the SS officer, he swung the big car round so that its boot was facing the door to the dormitory building and left the motor running in case they had to make a quick getaway. Thanks to the damned SS officer, such a situation now seemed highly likely.

He opened the boot and pretended to be busying himself with its contents, body half-hidden in its cavernous depths as they passed him.

'Spare the rod and spoil the child,' Schmitz was saying, face flushed quite hectically with excitement, as they continued to talk about this most delightful of subjects. 'I have always believed, my dear chap, in strict discipline – painfully strict discipline – for all ages.'

'Well, of course, it's your job, you being in the SS and all that,' Gore-Browne responded. He opened the door and said with unusual politeness for him. 'After you, *Hauptsturmbannführer*.' And then, in a hushed whisper that Otto just overheard, 'Show me the way to your private chamber!'

'No after *yow*, my dear old fellow,' Schmitz said in high-good humour, 'or do you wish to beat a retreat? Ha, ha!'

Laughing gaily, the two of them passed inside. Otto rose and grunted, 'Silly arseholes.'

A moment later the Count came puffing up, quite out of breath. Otto filled him in:

'They've gone up to his room, the SS officer's.'

'Oh dear,' the Count said mildly. As always he lived his roles; now he was a gentle priest.

'Oh dear, my arse!' Otto snarled. 'That SS sod has got a great big dirty pistol in his holster, I hope you know, and it looks like he's not afraid to use it! What now?'

The Count thought for a moment. 'We can't back down, Otto. Too much depends upon it. Our freedom depends on it!' He flashed a furtive look to left and right and then with a swift gesture, pulled something out of his sleeve.

Otto gasped. It was a big automatic pistol. The count started fumbling around, trying to load a clip the wrong way round.

'Jesus christ!' he cried, 'Give me that. Have you ever even used one of these things?' He snatched the pistol out of the Count's hand.

The Count seemed in no way offended. 'I've never been very good with short range weapons. In another life I was a crack shot with a sniper rifle. But my sleeve's hardly long

178

enough for one of those.' Hitching up his skirt like a fat woman tugging at the elastic of a pair of loose knickers, he pulled yet another, but smaller pistol from inside his waistband.

'Come on,' he said ignoring the look on Otto's face. 'Let's get in there and disturb the two love birds!'

Otto threw a last look in the big boot. Firing would soon have the whole god-forsaken place buzzing with SS men. They needed something quieter in the way of a weapon, if trouble started. He tucked the pistol in his belt and grabbed the length of thick rubber radiator hose and tyre iron that lay there. A moment later he was following the Count through the open door.

On tiptoe they crept down a still, grey corridor. Otto carried the tyre iron in one hand, the automatic pistol in the other, his heavy rubber hose stuffed into the well-pressed chauffeur trousers. The count was using both hands to hitch up his skirts. They listened at each door for the sound of voices, but hearing none until they came to the last. Otto held his finger to his lips in warning. There was someone talking inside. He pressed his mouth close to the Count's ear.

'I'll kick open the door. You go in with that pistol and Chrissake, *don't* take the safety off, you'll probably shoot yourself in the foot. All right, one, two, *three!*'

Otto's foot lashed against the door. It flew open. The Count tripped over his long black robe and nearly fell flat on his face.

Gore-Browne and Schmitz swung round in surprise. The cane that the latter had been demonstrating for the Englishman fell out of his hands, as he saw what looked like a mad priest with, a ladies' pearl-handled revolver in his well-manicured hand.

'*Urn Gotteswillen –*' Schmitz began, as Otto raised his tyre iron warningly. The cry of surprise turned to a simpering whisper, 'Oh, you're going to beat me... Oh, how *terrible!*'

He fell to his knees and to Otto's complete surprise raised his hands in the classic pose of supplication. 'How cruel you are! How terribly cruel... You *beast!*'

Otto, bewildered, kneed him in the face. Something snapped. Thick scarlet blood started to jet out of the officer's broken nose.

'Shut up, you silly dope!' he cried, and rounded on Gore-Browne, who was cowering behind a table laden with canes, switches, even a cricket bat.

The Count got to his feet, robe falling open to reveal shorter underskirts. 'It's him – GB,' he hissed, and flashing over with surprising speed, pulled out Schmitz's pistol from its holster.

Schmitz reeled back. 'You Catholic swine!' he breathed, splattering droplets of blood everywhere. 'I know you of the Inquisition! You are going to subject me to unspeakable tortures.' He quavered. 'I always knew it would end like this.' His words ended with a sudden groan, as Otto thwacked him over the head with the rubber tubing. He pitched face-forward onto the carpet and was still.

The Count turned his attention to the Englishman, who grasped the table edge like a surprised lion-tamer might when faced by a pride of his own animals in his own front-room.

'May I introduce myself?' he said with a formal bow. 'My name is Graf von der Weide. I have been empowered by your own authorities to rescue you from this place.'

'Rescue me?' Gore-Browne gasped and looked down at

the still handsome figure on the floor. 'But I like it here. I don't want to be rescued!'

'Bother. I was afraid you were going to say that,' the Count started.

'Let me at him,' Otto interrupted, and pushed the surprised aristocrat to one side. 'Listen, you pansy-arsed Tommy puff, you're going to be rescued whether you like it or not.'

Gore-Browne did not speak much German. Indeed he spoke no 'foreign' languages, save for a few 'technical terms' on the subject of sex (as he called them) in French, Italian, Spanish and German, but the threat was obviously there – and, besides, the blond young German in the smart grey chauffeur's uniform looked definitely very fetching. The tousled crop of blond hair, the strong nose, shapely cheekbones, well-toned body... Yes, he reminded Gore-Browne of some of his favourite past conquests. Plus chauffeurs, he knew from experience, were always very 'obliging'.

He lowered his hands from his face and said to the Count, though his eyes were still fixed on Otto. 'If I must, I must.'

'He must!' the Count repeated in German.

'You must!' Otto said and gave Gore-Browne a swift kick that propelled him towards the door, 'And damn quick. I'm not going back to any god-awful prison camp! Count, tell him what we're going to do to get him out of here.'

The door banged behind them as they fled.

On the floor, *Hauptsturmbannführer* Schmitz stirred and raised himself from the foetal position, which he had adopted in anticipation of further blows from the rubber truncheon. In spite of the painful throbbing of his broken nose, he was disappointed, very disappointed.

He had thought the young fellow in the chauffeur's uniform, who was undoubtedly extremely cruel, would have beaten him mercilessly. But nothing of the sort had happened. Now they had spirited away Gore-Browne, who might well have been the same kind of cruel-hearted English pervert as the chauffeur (he had been keenly interested in the canes, that was certain), and now he was all alone.

He heard the chauffeur slam home first gear and the car begin to move slowly across the courtyard. Suddenly he became aware of his own danger. For some reason or other, they were kidnapping Gore-Browne and they had spoken German with one another! Something strange was going on.

Abruptly it flashed through his mind that any failure on his part might well land him in the thick of it when the new fronts opened up; and in the trenches there was no place for his beloved canes. For some strange reason the average soldier had an antipathy against pain. He sprang to his feet and grabbed for the phone, gobs of bright red blood showering from his nose.

'Sergeant of the Guard,' he said thickly, 'Sergeant of the Guard, stop the big black Horch as soon–'

'What did you say?' the Guard-Commander asked, his speech slurred. He had demanded that there would only be one bottle between two men; the rest was for him to give to the Home for SS Widows. 'There's going to be none of this here drunken behaviour while I'm in charge! Bloody Papal Blessing indeed! Do you know that the Pope pisses in the sink?' Schmitz heard what sounded like gulping sounds straight out of a bottle. 'Eh?' the Guard-Commander finished.

'This is *Hauptsturmbannführer* Schmitz,' the SS officer said as clearly as he could through his stopped-up nose. 'I want you to stop the car presently heading in your direction.'

The sounds of a bottle smashing, general swearing, and the receiver being dropped. Then, 'Stop the car... Certainly, *Hauptsturm!* Immediately *Hauptsturm!* Regard it as already done, *Hauptsturm!*'

The Guard Commander banged down the phone and succeeded in smashing it through the cradle. Drunkenly he swayed to the window and flung it open, just as the rain came hissing down again.

'The priest,' he cried, his ears filled with the sudden roar of the high-powered motor. 'stop the pissing priest.'

Next instant he slumped to the floor, lying in the remains of his smashed bottle. 'I bet the sod didn't bless it after all!'

Otto swerved wildly round the corner, scattering Englishmen right and left. Ahead of him he could see the guard tumbling drunkenly out of the guardhouse, dropping their wine bottles and fumbling with their rifles as they did so. One of them was lowering the red-and-white-striped pole hastily.

'What are we going to do, Otto?' the Count cried in alarm from the back seat. 'They've been alerted!'

'Pray, Father Flynn!' Otto yelled above the snarl of the big motor and concentrated on the driving.

The first wild slug howled off the bonnet. Otto swerved violently to the right with shock and fought to control the great 8-cylinder automobile as it started to go into a skid on the slick wet cobbles. 'Hold tight!' he roared and ducked as a burst of machine-pistol fire ripped off the papal standard.

'I say,' the Count cried. 'Don't they know the Vatican is neutral?'

'Complain to the Pope!'

The distance between them and the firing guards was diminishing rapidly. Otto held onto the big wheel for all he was worth, wrenching the Horch from side to side crazily. The machine pistol gave another high-pitched hysterical scream. A line of gleaming silver holes stitched themselves the length of the bonnet and smashed the right windscreen pane. But now Otto was beyond caring. He was suddenly carried away by a wild, almost frenzied, surge of electric energy. He'd felt something similar that day in Holland when the mad little *Abwehr* agent Hirsch had been shot. Now nothing could stop him.

'Hold tight, Father Flynn,' he called once more. 'This is it!'

At eighty kilometres an hour, the Horch hit the pole. It burst apart, multi-coloured wood flying everywhere. A guard sprang out of the way a second too late. The bonnet struck him a tremendous blow. He went reeling into the ditch, machine-pistol chattering with the shock of that blow, slugs howling aimlessly into the grey dripping sky.

And then the Horch was careening wildly down the cobbled road, heading south into the gathering storm, in its boot an unconscious Gore-Browne; for that particular Englishman had fainted with fright at the first sounds of shooting.

'Give it some gas!' the Count yelled, as the first hard raindrops started to pelt down once more.

'What the devil do you think I'm doing?' Otto shouted back angrily, as they raced down the narrow cobbled road, swaying dangerously from side to side, the raindrops striking the interior through the broken windscreen like white flak.

'We'll head for Hamburg!' the Count cried, wiping the rain from his face. 'Through the village of Schwarzenbeck up ahead, onto Route Four, through Bergdorf and then into the city itself.'

'Right. But let's hope we get off these damn cobbles soon. They're knocking hell out of my kidneys!' Otto shouted back and then focussed on the road in front, peering, with his head bent over the wheel, through the cracked windscreen as the wipers whirred back and forth noisily, trying to keep the broken remains clear of the driving rain. *We're going to be very lucky to reach Hamburg today*, he told himself.

They roared into the red-brick village of Schwarzenbeck. There was no traffic, save for a few miserable cyclists. Otto took the S-bend around the grey-stone Gothic church, grey waves of water splashing up behind him and soaking an unfortunate rider. In the boot, Gore-Browne awoke from his faint and started to be sick. Among his many faults, he also had a weak stomach.

Otto hit the brakes and changed down. The yellow and black sign ahead indicated they were approaching Route Four, the main Berlin-Hamburg highway. To the left it ran to the capital; to the right to Hamburg. He flashed a look in his rear-view mirror. *Nothing!* They were not being followed. Good. He changed into second and started to take the road in the direction of Hamburg. Ahead of him the dreary dead-straight road seemed empty of human life. The heavy rain had obviously forced everybody under cover.

LEO KESSLER

But Otto was mistaken. Just as the village houses began to peter out, he saw a green-uniformed figure in the familiar black leather helmet of the *Schupos*. The figure was lumbering onto the road ahead through the grey fog of pelting rain, waving a red storm-lantern. And then, as Otto watched, more men joined the first to block the road. It was the *Schutzpolizei*.

'It's the bloody police!' he cried, jamming on the brakes.

The Horch screamed in protest. It shuddered to a violent stop, shimmying wildly. The Count, thrown out of his seat, was now sprawled in the rear footwell; a muffled yell came from the boot. For one awful moment, as the big car stood there blocking the road at a crazy angle, Otto thought he might have stalled the motor.

But no, he hadn't. It was still ticking over sweetly, despite the beating it had taken in their daring escape from the castle. For a moment he seemed mesmerized, but then as the *Schupos* started to run towards them, helmets gleaming in the rain, he realised the danger they were in.

He rammed home reverse. The Horch shot backwards, flinging the Count, who had just regained his seat, back into the footwell. The big car gathered speed, but its white-walled tyres suddenly slammed against the kerbstone. A chrome wheel hub cap clattered to the ground.

'Otto, chauffeurs don't normally drive like–' the Count started. Otto thrust home first and shot the car forward, and anything else the Count was going to say was knocked out of him. The manic chauffeur tore the wheel round, sweating and cursing angrily.

'*Halte! Oder wir schiessen!*' a bull cried.

' – like hooligans!' finished the Count from the back.

Otto ignored him, fighting the wheel furiously. He had to turn away from the *Schupos*. Hamburg was cut off. Berlin was now their only hope. The policemen were only fifty metres away, running towards them, fumbling with their clumsy leather pistol holsters.

Otto, the sweat streaming down his face, almost had the Horch round and facing in the direction of Berlin. The leading bull stopped. Standing there in the streaming rain in the middle of the road, he took aim as if he were on the police pistol range, one hand on his plump hip.

The cracks were deadened in the rain, but they still made Otto jump out of his skin. The bull was too agitated to aim correctly. All six of his bullets missed their target save the last one, which slammed, through the boot, missing Gore-Browne's head by inches, smashing a bottle of the red wine and splashing him with its contents.

'Oh my God,' he gasped inside the boot, 'I've been hit!' Once again he fell into a dead faint, as Otto thrust home first gear and went shooting up the road to Berlin, rocketing from side to side, leaving behind a trail of furious white water and several fat perspiring, impotent *Schupos*.

They were through the large village of Geesthacht now, barrelling along the road in the pouring rain, heading for the next small town of Lauenburg. To their right lay the River Elbe, glimpsed briefly through the flashing trees some hundred metres below the road. To their left, the fields, wet, miserable and very muddy, rose steeply so that anyone up there could have seen the whole length of the road. But the fields were empty of life, both animal and human. It was as if the big black car racing through the storm with its drenched, desperate occupants was alone in the world.

But in spite of their anxiety and their wet misery, Otto and the Count made hasty plans as they tore along Route Four. Originally they had planned to return with GB to the Count's house in Hamburg. Now that the road was barred, and after their experience in Schwarzenbeck, they reasoned that the whole countryside was probably being alerted. What were they going to do? As the Count expressed it: 'By the time we get to Lauenburg, Otto, we've got to have our decision. After it, there is the main road to Berlin and sooner or later they're going to stop us on it.'

Otto nodded his agreement, not taking his eyes off the road for an instant, his face greasy with rain-drops so that it looked as if he were sweating heavily.

'At Lauenburg there are two bridges across the Elbe and its arm, one for Berlin and the other across the main branch of the river taking the road to Luneburg.'

'Luneburg?' Otto asked sharply.

'Yes,' the Count saw his train of thought immediately. 'Very lonely heath country all the way to Luneburg itself. If we could get that far, we could ditch the car and make our way back to Hamburg by some other–' He stopped suddenly. 'Otto,' he gasped in abrupt alarm.

'What is it?'

'To the left! On the ridge line.'

Otto risked a swift glance. Above the fields, a silver car was hurtling along a parallel road at tremendous speed, a white V of spray shooting up behind it. And there could be only one reason that anyone would drive at that speed in this terrible weather. Otto put his foot down hard on the accelerator. The Horch shot forward with renewed vigour.

***

'There the criminals are!' Schmitz cried urgently from the passenger seat, his handsome face smeared with black, dried blood. He was staring like an eager hawk down over the fields to the Horch on the main road below. 'After them, driver! Give it all you've got!'

'I'm doing my best, *Hauptsturm*,' the driver protested above the whine of the straight-six engine, the roar of the wind and hiss of the tyres on the wet road. This was Lord Haw-Haw's personal car, a two-seater Wanderer with no roof.

'Do better!' Schmitz roared, as the Horch raced for Lauenburg, almost obscured by its wake.

The driver pressed his foot down. The green, glowing needle of the speedometer flicked upwards alarmingly. Now they were doing 120 kilometres an hour, nearly topping out the performance of the Wanderer roadster and a crazy speed for these conditions. The two-litre motor howled with the strain and every rivet whined to be freed from this impossible pressure.

Next to Schmitz, his companion, a young *Sonderführer*, MP-40 machine pistol in his lap, the only man sober enough to accompany him in the chase, turned an ashen-green with fear. At this speed they were heading for catastrophe.

Schmitz didn't notice. His mind was completely bound up with his new friend who had been kidnapped so abruptly from right under his nose, just as they were beginning to become acquainted. He wanted him back.

'There's a crossroads a quarter of a kilometre up the road,' he yelled at the *Sonderführer*. 'Beat them to it, driver! There's three days' special leave if you get there before them and block the road.' He leaned forward, his battered face gleaming with excitement, as if he were physically urging the silver roadster forward. The Wanderer raced on….

'…They're pulling away from us!' Otto yelled urgently above the strong throbbing of the Horch's engine. Ahead of them he could just make out the green copper-covered dome of Lauenburg's church.

'I see them,' the Count yelled, his face streaming with rain from the broken windscreen, and started winding down his rear window.

'What are you going to do, you silly old bastard?' Otto yelled, feeling yet more wet, icy air blasting the back of his neck, but not daring to take his eyes off the road for one moment now.

Ever resourceful, the Count bravely pulled the small ladies' pistol out of his skirt. He clicked off the safety.

'They won't take us alive, Otto,' he said grimly, and fired.

The bullet hit the muddy field a couple of hundred metres below the other road and a rabbit, which just happened to be sheltering from the driving rain, scuttled deeper into cover, wondering if the hunting season had not begun rather early this year.

Otto started to come to the first little fishermen cottages which lined the entrance to the small town of Lauenberg. The Wanderer was roaring down towards the crossroads now and he saw that if he were not quicker, it would reach the junction ahead of him. Desperately, he pressed the accelerator down the floorboard. He had to make it!

Out of nowhere, a dog ran across the road. Instinctively he braked. The Horch spun right round on the slick surface, turning a full clock face until it careered to a stop. The Count yelled and was nearly flung through his open window. In the boot Gore-Browne was sick once more, and with a sinking heart Otto saw that the silver roadster had skidded to a body-trembling halt at the crossroads. A man in black uniform was doubling out of it, crouching low as he ran, machine-pistol at the ready. They were cut off from the bridges across the Elbe.

Then he saw it. A small, steep, cobbled path leading down to the Elbe below. Otto didn't hesitate. He rammed home first gear in the same instant that the dark-uniformed figure opened fire. Slugs zipped along the length of wet tarmac. Little blue spurts of flame erupted, hurrying towards them with frightening speed. And then the car lurched forward.

The rear window shattered, cracking into a gleaming spider's web, showering a shocked Count with glass fragments. Next moment the Horch was slithering and slipping down the narrow path, branches slapping into both sides, scratching at the paintwork, blinding Otto with green foliage time and time again, as he fought to keep the big car on the road, ears already full of the roar of the Wanderer's motor as it took up the chase once more.

'They can't get by that way!' Schmitz yelled triumphantly. 'There's only a tow-path down there, leading into the dock. There's no clear road. I know it well,'

'What now?' the *Sonderführer* gasped, hurriedly fitting another magazine as the open-top roadster leapt over the height and started slithering down the narrow cobbled path in pursuit.

'What now?' Schmitz echoed, now in the driver's seat.

'Why we trap them down there. There's no way out.' He let out a strained maniacal laugh over the steering wheel. '*Sonderführer* Ziemann, they're finished this time!'

Beside him, Ziemann told himself that all SS officers were crazy. One false move on the descent and they'd slide right into the Elbe, and somehow he didn't think they'd have much chance of swimming away if the one-ton Wanderer hit the water at this height. And even if they did, Lord Haw-Haw would have their guts for garters when he learned that his private car was permanently out of action. He bit his bottom lip and felt the sweat begin to break out all over his body.

Otto swerved right off the track. With a crunch of rending metal and a tinkle of glass breaking, the Horch came to rest in a clump of bushes, its headlights shattered, the right mudguard crumpled like a banana-skin.

'What are you going to do, Otto?' the Count cried in alarm, his chin bleeding from the shattered glass.

'Shut up! Keep still!' Otto commanded. He kicked open the door and vaulted out of the driver's seat, pistol already in his hand.

The pursuing car was still invisible on the path above him, hidden from view by the dripping foliage and the squalls of grey rain, but Otto could hear it well enough, as the unknown driver fought it down the ascent, his motor roaring away in first gear. He tensed. He knew he would only get one chance, but he knew too he had no exact idea of how he might stop their pursuer, and at the same time ensure that the path was free to use again.

There was only room for one car on it and he would have to climb up it once more if they were going to get to

Lauenburg. Should he just hold them up? Or shoot the driver and hope for the best? *Blast it, what am I going to do?*

Suddenly the gleaming silver Wanderer was there, slithering in the mud, the two areas cleared by the wipers on the windscreen looking down at him like baleful, glaring eyes.

Otto hesitated no longer. He aimed. The pistol jerked in his hand. The windscreen disappeared in a mass of cracked glass. He thought he heard a thin scream of utter fear, but later could never be sure that it had not been his imagination. Suddenly the roadster was completely out of control, thrashing wildly through the vegetation, the driver clutching at his shoulder, the other man trying desperately to control the wheel. Otto dived to one side.

The beautiful silver roadster swung by, gathering speed, and then it was out in the air, riding up and up, flying outwards, its wheels still spinning, its straight-six running strong and free at last, the screams of the two men inside it clearly audible.

Otto dropped the pistol to his side, mouth open in awed amazement, as the Wanderer began to drop at an alarming rate. Nothing could save it now. He closed his eyes, then opened them again. Why didn't they get out? But already it was too late for that. The car, all twenty-odd hundredweight of it, hit the river. A tremendous jet of water erupted into the grey wet sky. For one moment Otto thought it might stay on the surface so that its occupants could get out. But that wasn't to be. There was a mad flurry of bubbles. Water sprayed up on both sides. One last obscene belch of trapped air and then it was gone, the only sign of its passing: the ever widening ripple of water and the loud echoing silence, disturbed only by the hiss of the rain.

***

'Die Heide at last,' the Count announced, breaking the gloomy silence which had existed in the battered car ever since they had crossed the bridge at Lauenburg. Its left rear tyre was now almost down to its rim, so that the whole affair bumped along like a short-legged beggar, its occupants still preoccupied with what had happened down at the Elbe.

Otto braked and the car creaked wearily to stop, its engine continuing to shudder for a few seconds after he had turned off the ignition.

'What now?' he asked and slumped back wearily in his seat.

It had stopped raining and now the moor sparkled, with the raindrops glistening on the purple-green heather.

'I think we'd better have a look at our guest, Otto,' the Count said. He hitched up his damp skirts and crawled stiffly out of the car, while Otto shifted awkwardly in his damp uniform and then decided to do the same.

Wearily, he stamped his feet on the road and stared around at the moor stretching to the horizon, broken only by lines of skinny fir trees and the drainage ditches cut into the landscape. It would be a good place to get rid of the car, which somehow he suspected they would have to do: for with it they would have stood out in any inhabited place. One tyre virtually flat, windscreen cracked and shattered, rear window smashed by gunfire, two lengths of silver bullet-holes running along its body – *No officer, that's how I bought it*, imagined Otto, a little of his old wit returning.

'Otto, our guest,' the Count's voice broke into his thoughts.

He turned. The Count was supporting GB, who still

looked very green, and who creaked at every joint as he was helped along.

'What?' he began to croak.

'Have no fear, my dear Mister Honourable,' the Count interrupted him gently. 'You are among friends.'

'Friends?' Gore-Browne spluttered.

'Yes,' the Count reached in the car and brought out his silver flask. 'Here, a drink of this will do you good. May I introduce myself? I do love introducing myself.'

He straightened up and put on his 'man of destiny' face, which he practised every morning in front of his shaving mirror. 'Graf von der Weide at your service! Sent here to rescue you by your illustrious and noble father er – Colonel Warden!' Without taking his dark eyes, standing out of his head like hard-boiled eggs, off the haggard Englishman drinking the cognac, he added, 'And this is my great friend, Herr Otto Stahl.'

Gore-Browne lowered the flask, colour returning to his cheeks. 'Rescue me, you said?'

'Yes,' the Count repeated proudly.

'But I don't want to be res –' Gore-Browne started to protest, then his eye fell on the young chauffeur and he stopped abruptly. In spite of his soaked, somewhat bedraggled, appearance, the young chap was definitely very handsome. Fine blue eyes and a mop of bright blond hair, good physique. He summed up the situation at once. His 'great friend' the old man had called his chauffeur. Highly significantly. But then chauffeurs, he always maintained, were always very obliging even if they didn't have very much in the way of 'soul'.

'What are you going to do with me?' he asked, 'Now

LEO KESSLER

you've got me, I mean.' He took another swig of the flask.

The Count beamed and flashed Otto a significant look.

'Now that's the spirit,' he said. 'I'm sure your illustrious father would esteem it highly. Where we are going? Why, to Greece, my dear fellow. Athens, to be precise.'

'Athens,' Gore-Browne brightened up appreciably. He *knew* the Greeks. 'I've heard there are some awfully nice chaps down there. By plane, I suppose. It will be awfully nice to get out of this dreary place. I mean Germany does do a bally nice job with its soldiers, marching, and bands and all that – almost as good as the Guards – but the weather.' He gave an affected shrug. 'Absolutely impossible.'

Otto shook his head. What with the Count posturing and this Tommy warm-brother flapping his pinkies around, as if he were waving a lace handkerchief, this was turning out like ladies' night in the Turkish baths; didn't the silly affected buggers realise that there was the *Gestapo* on their tails? He harrumphed, noisily.

'The jolly old tavernas, ouzo, retsina and a warm Aegean breeze by tonight, what?' Gore-Browne was saying happily.

'Well, not quite,' the Count said hesitantly.

'What's the plan now, then?' Otto snapped, speaking in harsh German. 'The registration number of the car was entered in the log-book of the guardhouse as we entered the castle. You can be shit-sure that they'll trace your address in Hamburg from that quick enough. The big boys in the leather overcoats will be waiting for us there, you can take poison on that, Count.'

'Agreed, agreed, my dear boy,' the Count said, not looking unduly worried. He gazed from face to face and said in English again. 'We are a rather strange trio, are we not? A priest who is not one, though he would dearly love to have the blessing of our Mother Church one of these days. A chauffeur in the same situation, and an Englishman of noble birth, who isn't exactly – er – what he seems to be.'

'Oh get on with it,' Otto snorted.

The Count reached inside his damp skirt and pulled out what looked a heavy, waterlogged sock and then another. 'Though we have a long, long journey in front of us,' he said slowly, weighing the strange objects, 'possibly full of danger, I think these little fellows will ensure that we arrive safely.' He opened the top of one of the socks and poured a stream of gold coins on to his palm. 'The Horsemen of Saint George, your patron saint, my dear Gore-Browne. They will be our – er – chargers for the long crusade southwards.'

Gore-Browne's plump face fit up, the word 'danger' forgotten, suddenly full of enthusiasm. 'Oh, I say, a bit of an adventure you mean, rather like the scouts.' Gore-Browne had always had a soft spot for scouts. 'Should be great fun, especially with two stout chaps like you, er, Count and Otto!' He fluttered his sandy eyelashes coyly at a disgusted Otto. 'You speak the lingo, know the best places to eat, I suppose, and all that!' He clapped his hands together in schoolgirlish delight. 'Oh, this is really going to be fun!'

BOOK 3 – ON THE RUN

CHAPTER 1

The slow train chugged through the hilly landscape. In the distance the mountains were capped with snow, for in Upper Austria it had been a long, cold winter. It was still dark and by lifting his carriage window's blackout blind, a weary Otto could see the orange sparks flying from the engine like red-hot sawdust, though already the sun was beginning to flush the sky a pale pink, against which the peaks stood out a stark, jagged inky-black.

He let the blind fall again and reaching over for the Thermos of coffee which they had bought at Innsbruck, unscrewed the cap, and poured himself a lukewarm cupful of the stuff. Opposite him on the wooden bench, the Count and GB propped up against each other in a rough pyramid, snored in unison.

'Faces that only a mother could love,' Otto commented sourly and savoured the warmth given off by the coffee as he gulped it down his gullet.

They had been travelling for two days now, ever since they had abandoned the car, and tramped into Luneburg, wandering around the dingy little suburbs of the place until they found what Otto sought: a workers' pawnshop where he had bought them three rough suits from a pawnbroker, who looked very Jewish indeed, although he greeted them with the usual '*Heil Hitler*' and draped his skinny hunchback-frame with the chocolate-brown uniform of the SA.

The long train journey to Munich and from there across the old border with Austria (non-existent since Austria had become the 'Eastern March' in Nazi parlance) had been uneventful, save for two things: the number of troops who seemed to be moving southwards – twice they had been held up by long troop-trains carrying tanks and guns into Austria; and GB's mild attempt at importuning in the male toilet of Munich's *Hauptbahnhof*, where they had gone for a quick wash and brush-up.

'I was only trying to help you with your fly buttons, Otto,' he apologized lamely in faulty German, 'I thought they seemed a bit stiff.' To which Otto had replied sourly, 'Yes, and I bet they weren't the only things that were stiff. Hands off, Englishman, or you'll be lacking a set of ears!' Although Otto was quite sure the Englishman had not understood the German, he had comprehended well enough what Otto's clenched fist had meant. Thereafter he had left Otto in peace, though now and again he caught GB throwing him interested glances with much fluttering of those sandy eyelashes.

Now, as they crawled ever closer to the Italian frontier with the Third Reich, which, according to the Count, was well guarded, they began to change trains more frequently, moving twenty kilometres or so in one and then transferring to yet another wooden-seated local, which stopped at every God-forsaken little hamlet and village. The time had passed leadenly, and Otto commented more than once, 'They even stop to let the cows cross the track on this service.'

'It is typical old-world Austrian courtesy,' the Count had soothed him and GB had added eagerly, 'I once knew some Austrian chaps – frightfully decadent they were!'

Now it would soon be dawn and Otto knew they were slowly approaching the border, but before they reached that pass, they would get off and meet the Count's mysterious contact, who supposedly would guide them across the mountains into Italy.

Otto hoped that for once the Count would not make a mess of it; for he had no illusions of what would happen to them, or at least to him and the Count, if they fell into the hands of the *Gestapo*. It would be a bullet in the back of the head in some evil, dark torture-cellar.

Hurriedly he forgot that unpleasant possibility and, finishing the coffee, raised the blackout blind once more to stare at the dawn countryside, flushing ever more rapidly in the light of the ascending sun which hung like a blood-red ball on the peaks, great black shadows racing across the fields like the shadows of gigantic crows. He craned his neck a little and followed the progress of the black locomotive, as it puffed up the curving incline, ever deeper into the foothills which would soon give way to the Border Mountains, trailing thick white clouds of smoke behind it.

Suddenly he forgot the train. To his left, parked along a dusty white country road, hidden by the big oaks that lined one side of it, there was tank after tank, black, sinister and immensely powerful, with, crouched around them, little groups of soldiers boiling their morning coffee around flickering little petrol fires or lazily eating pieces of hard bread, while here or there an officer or NCO strode by officiously, clipboard in hand.

Automatically Otto started to count the tanks; there was nothing better to do anyway. But by the time he had reached fifty, the little local train passed into a tunnel through the hills and when it emerged again, the road and its tanks had vanished.

Otto sat back against the hard wooden bench, puzzled. What were so many tanks doing out here in this remote Upper Austrian valley? From his training with the *Abwehr* spy school back in '39, he knew that fifty tanks meant he had something in the way of a whole regiment out there. Where could they be going? After all, ahead lay Italy, and Mussolini's Italy was Hitler's ally.

Perhaps they were out on manoeuvres, he told himself in the end, though he knew quite well that troops didn't usually manoeuvre over farmland, at least not in a friendly country – and Hitler's own homeland to boot! It was all very strange.

'The hamlet of Klein Hohental,' the Count announced. 'Headquarters of the NNSPfRG.'

'The what?' Otto exclaimed, peering around at the wood-frame station with its sagging platform and the tarnished, but clearly visible, double-eagle plaque of the old Austro-Hungarian Empire above the ticket office. Somewhere a cock crowed and drowned the last sounds of the train disappearing now up the track into the mountains.

'The Neo-National Socialist Party for the Regeneration of Germany,' the Count said, finishing the last of the coffee, while Gore-Browne stared open-mouthed at the place. 'They've got at least fifty members now.'

'But we've already got a National Socialist Party,' Otto objected, carefully avoiding the hole in the wooden platform, beneath which a herd of skinny black pigs rooted hopefully, 'with nine million members.'

'I know, Otto. But you see, Carlo Ernesto Streithammer doesn't agree with Herr Hitler. He thinks he's too left-wing. Besides, he strongly objects to the *Führer*'s policy in the South-Tirol, over there.' With a nod of his head, he indicated the snow-capped Brenner shimmering now in the warm spring sunshine.

Otto looked puzzled. Out of habit Gore-Browne strolled over to the black-tarred 'piss-corner' at the far end of the rickety platform to look at the graffiti on it. He bent his head this way and then that, obviously looking for something that was beyond Otto's comprehension.

'Let me explain,' the Count said, tossing away the thermos which was their only luggage. 'I first got to know him when I worked for the *Abwehr* at the time of the Pact of Steel, Mussolini and Hitler's deal back in the 30s.

Streithammer had hoped that South Tirol, his homeland, would be united with Germany, of whose National Socialist Party he was a loyal member. Instead, Hitler promised the *Duce* he would respect Italy's claim to the mainly German-speaking population of the South-Tirol. Immediately Streithammer left the Nazi Party, went into exile here, formed his own grouping and since then fought both the Nazis on this side of the border and the Fascists on that.'

'With fifty members?' Otto said cynically, as Gore-Browne did a sort of headstand in order to be able to read some particularly interesting piece of graffiti.

'All the villages are with him on both sides of the border.' The Count frowned at some memory or other. 'Herr Streithammer is a very violent man, very violent indeed.'

'How do you mean, Count?'

'You'll see,' Graf von der Weide said darkly. 'You'll see.'

They trudged down the dusty street between dirty-white houses, long lines of last year's maize-cobs and bundles of parched tobacco leaves hanging from beneath carved wooden balconies like dried-up bats. Skinny, bare-footed children played in the gutters, and a lone cow wandered by, head weighed down as if by the bell at its throat, which tolled miserably. A few chickens scratched the barren earth, dust flying from their feathers in thick clouds every time they hopped out of the way of strangers.

'Don't look as if they've got a pot to piss in,' Otto commented.

'It's one of the poorest areas in Western Europe,' the Count agreed.

'I suppose the young chaps here would be grateful for a couple of coppers,' Gore-Browne said hopefully.

'Yes, I suppose they would,' the Count said a little absently. 'For the most part they keep afloat by farming and, more importantly, smuggling across the Austro-Italian border. Human beings into Italy, goods such as coffee into the Reich.'

For a few moments more they walked in silence down the village street, past the onion-towered baroque church into a cobbled square, village pump holding pride of place, piles of dried-up animal droppings everywhere. The Count stopped and pointed to the inn at the far end decorated with the usual flags and green garlands.

'*Gasthaus zur Linde*,' he said. 'Party Headquarters. Come on!'

As the three of them got closer they could hear the clash and thump of a brass band belting out the *Bademoeiler*, a marching tune to the bombastic tones of which the *Führer* had always made his dramatic pre-war appearances at the Nuremberg Party Rallies. And just like at those rallies, this *Bademoeiler* was accompanied at regular intervals by the strangely distorted sound of thousands of voices crying fanatically '*Sieg Heil, Sieg Heil unserem Führer!*'

Otto looked questioningly at the Count. 'I thought you said he had only fifty followers. That sounds like fifty thousand!'

'It does seem strange, Otto,' the Count agreed.

They opened the squeaky door which hung on one hinge and were confronted by the typical Upper Austrian inn-interior: curved wooden chairs in little alcoves, a fly-blown picture of a little boy urinating into the usual puddle and the grim warning, '*DON'T DRINK WATER*', a zinc-covered bar, a ceiling-high green-tiled oven, and the inevitable pretzels hanging from little wooden stands on each table like criminals from gallows. But it was none of these things that caught their open-mouthed attention.

It was the trio at the far end of the room before the huge mirror.

On one side a sickly handsome, barefoot youth turned the handle of an ancient horn-gramophone from which issued the blare of the *Badenweiler*. On the other, a white-haired, toothless hag produced the cheering from a similar instrument. In their midst, posing dramatically in front of the mirror, hands raised in an impressively theatrical gesture, mouth curling and snarling in soundless passion, stood a tremendous man, bulging out of his chocolate-coloured uniform, his quiff and toothbrush moustache an exact imitation of those affected by the *Führer*, save for one thing, his were a bright, flaming red!

'Carlo Ernesto Streithammer,' the Count announced simply, as the huge man spun round to stare at the strangers with baleful, red eyes. '*Führer* of the Neo-National Socialist Party for the Regeneration of Germany.'

Otto took a quick look at those little red eyes, and thick neck like that of a Prussian corporal, the hands like small steel-shovels and a face that had taken much hammering in its time, and told himself he wouldn't like to eat cherries with Carlo Ernesto Streithammer. The winders stopped winding, and the records slowed down to a halt. For a moment, a tense and dangerous silence blanketed the room.

Suddenly, the big man moved forward. Advancing on the Count, face set in a tough grimace, he clicked abruptly to attention and shot out his right hand. 'Heil Streithammer!' he bellowed so that the wooden walls seemed to shake.

'Heil Streithammer!' the Count answered, raising his right arm and saluting the figure towering above him somewhat lamely. Next instant they were in each other's arms, slapping one another on the back heartily, the Count gasping as if in the last throes of a fatal asthma attack each time the giant struck him.

Otto breathed a sigh of relief. Streithammer was on their side.

'So that communist traitor is still in power in Berlin, eh?' Streithammer growled, recovering from what was apparently his daily speech-making practice before the mirror in front of a litre pot of beer.

The Count nodded, sipping his own beer slowly, while

Gore-Browne smiled winningly at the sickly handsome youth who brought it. 'I bet that kid would be glad of a pair of shoes, the poor chap. Pathetically grateful, I shouldn't wonder,' the Englishman added to Otto.

'Depends on the price,' Otto commented, and concentrated on the giant.

Streithammer was talking. 'Our day will come – Berlin and in Rome. Look what the swine over the other side did to me last spring when they caught me near the Brenner!' He ripped open his tight shirt and bared his massive chest.

They craned their heads to pick out the letters scarred among the tangled jungle of red hair that covered Streithammer's chest.

'O... V... R... A,' the Count deciphered the word for them. '*Organizzione Vigilanza Repressione Antifascismo.*'

'Exactly,' the big man said grimly. 'Their secret police. Four of them held me down and burnt it on my chest with cigarettes, then they locked me in a barn near the frontier and said they were going to cut my eggs and tail off next morning. The sphaghetti-eaters are always threatening sexed-up things like that.'

The Count shuddered dramatically.

'But the Macaroni who wants to fix Streithammer has to get up early in the morning,' the big man said and his leathery face cracked into a smile. 'I strangled the guard at the door just before dawn and battered the other three to death with a shovel while they slept.' He took a huge swallow of beer, the suds forming a white beard and moustache, making his lips gleam a bright-red as if he had just dipped them in blood. 'Four OVRA fewer.'

The Count turned to the other two. 'The OVRA's

Mussolini's equivalent of the *Gestapo*,' he explained quickly in English for GB's sake. 'You'll find them in every town and village the length and breadth of Italy, but they are especially thick on the ground in the South-Tirol on account of the German-speaking population. That's why we've got to be especially careful over the next part of our journey.'

He turned back to Streithammer and said, '*Mein Führer*, I would like to make a sizeable contribution to Party funds – in gold.'

Streithammer's red eyes gleamed at the mention of gold.

'If you could get us across the frontier into Italy,' The Count went on to explain how once they had crossed the frontier they would take local buses out of the frontier zone till they reached the chief city of the South-Tirol, Bolzano. From there they would take the coastal train to Genoa, where they hoped to catch one of the ferries down through the Adriatic Sea to Athens.

Up to that point, the giant had listened in attentive silence; in spite of his bulk and pretensions, he was obviously no fool.

'Not on!' he objected. 'No more ferries going from there to Greece.'

'Why?' the Count asked quickly.

'I don't know, Count. Something's in the air. There have been *Wehrmacht* convoys through here twice this week, but what the meaning for it is? Well that's beyond me.' He saw the Count's disappointed look and said quickly. 'Don't worry, you can always get across to Yugoslavia – Dubrovnik, Split, or somewhere like that and work your way from there to Greece. But that's *your* problem. Mine is to get you across the frontier.' He rubbed the foam off his brilliant red moustache and sucked his teeth thoughtfully.

'There'll be a moon tonight, crescent moon,' he said, as if he were considering all the possibilities, 'but by four in the morning, it shouldn't be so bright any more. Hmm. All right, we'll set out at midnight.' He turned his attention to Otto and Gore-Browne for the first time and didn't seem particularly impressed.

'It's going to be a long haul,' he said. 'Better get some vittels inside you, and plenty of shuteye.' He added, 'There isn't much room in the village. You'll have to double up. You stay with me. You–'

But before he could say any more, Gore-Browne interrupted the giant. In his best German, he said, 'Could I have that party-comrade, please,' he pointed to the sickly-handsome youth.

The giant shrugged. 'As far as I'm concerned. But I warn you, he's got fleas.'

An excited Gore-Browne dismissed the issue, and said in English. 'Fleas. How delightfully perverse – and what an adventure! Not a bit like Shaftesbury Avenue.' And with that enigmatic remark, the discussion ended.

The old woman with the goitre under her chin had finished feeding Otto. He had spent the entire meal looking at that growth, looking like an extra breast hanging where her neck should have been. He had gazed at it, spilling his soup down his stubbly face, and excusing himself every time it happened. Now it was time to turn in. There were still four hours till midnight and Streithammer had insisted they should all get some sleep before they embarked on the rugged ascent into

Italy.

With a crooked finger, the old woman indicated he should follow her. He gulped. Leading him by the flickering light of an old petroleum lamp – for the village possessed no electricity, nor running water for that matter – she clambered wearily up the creaking wooden stairs and opened the door to a bedroom. It was completely filled by a great double-bed, covered with a lumpy feather quilt so that it looked as if a skinny white elephant rested on the sagging springs.

'Sleep,' she said and went out.

Gratefully, and not without a certain relief, he began to take off his clothes. He hadn't slept at all in the train. Suddenly he felt absolutely exhausted. With a sigh of relief, clad only in his shirt, he clambered into the sagging bed and closed his eyes. But not for long.

Minutes later the old woman returned, still bearing her petroleum lamp. Now she was clad in an old-fashioned nightgown and her scraggy hair was tied up in white rag curlers. Otto opened his weary eyes.

'Anything wrong, granny?'

She shook her head and gave him a toothless smile. Putting the lamp on the other side of the bed, she clambered in beside an astonished Otto.

'Hey,' he cried, 'what's going on?'

'Nuffing,' she croaked. 'I've had none o' dat kind of piggery dese fifty years.' She settled her goitre more comfortably on the blue-and-white checked pillow. 'You can put out de light, if you would be so kind, gracious gentleman.'

'Put out the light,' Otto stuttered. 'But you don't mean–'

His words were drowned by a tremendous fart. The old

woman sighed happily; a moment later she was snoring mightily. With a groan, Otto got out of bed and put his trousers back on.

Miserably, Otto wandered through the deserted village. Everyone else, it seemed, was fast asleep, though from somewhere or other he could hear the faint strains of *Wiener Blut*, obviously a record being played on one of those two ancient gramophones from the inn. He grunted hard and told himself that he knew who Gore-Browne would be waltzing with – and where.

He walked on, the sounds of Strauss's waltz dying away altogether. Now everything was silence save for the rustle of the wind in the trees on both sides of the village street.

Ahead, in the silver glow of the crescent moon, he could make out the stark jagged outline of the mountain peaks that marked the border with Italy they would soon have to cross.

He stopped and stared up at them. How remote they seemed in that spectral light. Suddenly Otto Stahl was overcome by strong feelings of sadness, relief, and excitement. He was being forced to leave his homeland yet once again, but this time on an adventure that would lead him to a new and better life. If what the Count had said about the Reich was correct, the war would be over soon. Then they could both finally go back home. But in the mean-time, he might just be able to cope with a few months on the Greek coast.

He turned and started to walk back, disappearing into the rich darkness, wondering what the morrow might bring.

CHAPTER 2

'Heil Streithammer!' the assembled villagers cried, arms held out stiffly, as their guide, followed by the three strangers, passed through the double-line of them – there was even a barefoot young woman, a fat baby held at her naked right breast, but with her arm raised dutifully in salute to their *Führer*.

Gravely, the giant acknowledged their greeting, striding forward like Hitler himself, flapping his right arm at regular intervals. Behind him, Gore-Browne blew a loving kiss at the sickly youth.

'How was the dance, eh?' Otto asked in stunted English.

'Lean closer and I'll tell you,' replied GB.

Otto replied in German. 'What, so you can offload your fleas onto me? Not likely!'

Streithammer swung round at the edge of the village, big hands set on his hips, legs spread apart. He puffed out his chest, and declared imperiously, 'Comrades, I leave you once again to venture into enemy territory. Remember your duty. Remain loyal and true.'

A woman sobbed and in the silver light, Otto could see that several of the poverty-stricken villagers were dabbing their eyes, as if a little overcome by emotion.

'Heil Streithammer!' the giant bellowed at the top of his voice.

'Heil Streithammer!' the villagers cried back. In a barn a cock started to crow in sudden alarm, as if the bird had missed dawn and he had failed to do his duty. To its crowing, the party set off, heading for the mountains.

By two o'clock that morning they were climbing steadily, with no one saying very much. They all knew they would be wise to save their breath for the two-thousand-metre ascent ahead. Their track was very narrow, though in no way dangerous, for the moonlight was bright enough for them to see what they were doing. Their breath came in little puffs of smoke: the air was icy and Otto was glad they were moving relatively fast; it would have been too cold otherwise.

An hour later, Streithammer allowed them ten minutes' rest in the cover of some snow-covered firs. Taking a drink of water from a small mountain pool, Otto gasped with shock. It was so cold that it struck him an almost physical blow, making his head ache.

'From now onwards,' Streithammer lectured them as they lay gratefully on the ground, resting their aching calf-muscles, 'we don't stop until we reach the Italian side. The Macaronis put their best troops up here on the frontier to impress that Bolshevik Hitler, and one doesn't play games with the *Alpini* – they know their mountains. Besides the OVRA also run patrols around here to make sure the soldiers don't slack.' He looked around at them with his little red eyes. 'Comrades, from now onwards it's *marschieren oder kreprieren.*'

'What did he say?' GB asked not understanding the thick South-Tirolean dialect.

'March or croak,' the Count translated, his voice subdued.

'Patrol!' Streithammer hissed abruptly. 'Look!' he ducked, and automatically the others followed suit.

Down below, some two hundred metres away, a group of six soldiers were leading a train of laden mules spread out in a slow thoughtful line up the mountainside, plodding ever upwards, as if they could go on like that for days, in spite of the tremendous loads on their backs.

'Sacrament!' Streithammer cursed, as they watched the *Alpini*, the elite Italian mountain troops disappear into a canyon.

'What's the matter, *Führer*?' the Count asked apprehensively.

'Supply patrol,' Streithammer answered, not answering before he was sure there was not another file of mules following.

'Does that bode ill for the true cause?'

'Hmm, it means they've established a new lookout post in the mountains that I don't know about.' The man who was going to regenerate National Socialism cursed and spat angrily on the hard rock. 'That means we can't use the old route, in case they're watching it. We'll have to go higher.'

'How high?' the Count asked, looking at the others.

'The snow-line. We'll have to go up to the snow-line.'

'Oh dear,' the Count said. 'Ah, um...'

'Oh god-damn bloody dear indeed!' Otto cursed angrily. 'If there's nothing we can do?' He glanced at Streithammer, and the other swung his head from side to side. 'Come on, let's get on with it.'

For the next two hours, they climbed silently, the ascent

to each fresh height a reminder that yet another one lay before them. Their big guide did not allow them to stop, even when Gore-Browne staggered more and more wildly.

In the end, when the Englishman gasped he couldn't go another step, Streithammer grunted angrily and simply slung him over his shoulder, as if he were light as air. Together the illegitimate son of England's leader and the future one of a regenerated Germany marched on.

As it began to grow light, the peaks sparkling a warm pink in the ascending sun, they finally started to descend, their legs feeling as if they were made of soft rubber, so that time and time again, Otto and the Count slipped and tripped over the slightest obstruction.

At six, Streithammer slipped a refreshed Gore-Browne from his massive shoulder and allowed them to stop for a minute, while he gave them their instructions for the final stage of the crossing.

'We're through the *Alpini* lines now,' he growled, picking his nose, as if he were bored with the whole business. 'Roughly about two and half kilometres inside Italy itself.' He took his finger out his nostril and pointed down the hillside. 'See that little road down there? That leads into the first village where you can catch the nine o'clock bus to Bolzano. I shall take you that far and then you're on your own. Got it?'

The three of them nodded and the Count said a little apprehensively, 'There'll be no checking of documents down in the village? It is near the frontier, after all.'

Streithammer simply shook his head.

'But what about the villagers?' Otto asked. 'I mean we'll stick out like a sore thumb down there, surely. It won't be every day that they see strangers like us.'

Streithammer gave one of his rare smiles. His face seemed to crack in two. 'They'd know better than to betray friends of the *Führer.*' He doubled that massive fist of his. 'Because if they did they'd be lacking a set of teeth in double-quick time. Clear?'

'Clear,' they echoed as one.

They continued.

'OVRA!' Streithammer gasped. 'Hit the dirt!'

With surprising speed for such a big man, he dropped into the dried-up drainage ditch at the side of the road, the others following him in. A second later, a black Fiat tourer swung round the bend and started to slow down, with a crash and thunder of gears being forced home clumsily.

'How do you know it's them?' Otto hissed, peeping over the top of the ditch and taking in the black car with its pretentious radiator design and row of unnecessary lamps on a gleaming bumper.

'Down this way, only the Militia and the OVRA have cars,' Streithammer replied. 'All the peasants have in the way of wheeled transport is the family ox-cart. They –' He broke off abruptly. The Fiat had stopped!

It was parked about a hundred metres away from their position. A small Italian got out from the passenger door, black-felt hat pulled down over one eye, collar of his trench coat pulled up high, a cigarette hanging out of the corner of his thin-lipped mouth.

'I say – Humphrey Bogart.' Gore-Browne whispered.

'Pipe down there!' the Count hissed.

In tense silence the four of them watched the little Italian, who did look a little like the Hollywood gangster they remembered from pre-war films. He removed his cap and surveyed the heights with a pair of binoculars, swinging them back and forth as if he were searching for something in particular.

'Look at the bulge under his armpit!' Streithammer whispered. 'He's OVRA all right. That's a hand cannon he's got there.'

'But what do they want?' the Count asked.

'They're looking for us. There's no doubt about that,' Streithammer answered, a worried frown on his big ugly face. 'Wait, he's getting back in. Everyone down!'

The little man hopped back into the black Fiat, the driver let out the clutch and he crawled by them before stopping once again to allow the little man a repeat performance.

'What now?' Otto asked. 'If they can't find us like this, they'll just stake out the village. They'll pick us up if we try to board the bus.'

'You're right there,' Streithammer agreed and then suddenly his face lit up. 'Count,' he said to the older man, 'what would it be worth to you to be able to travel to the coast in your own private vehicle? I mean, how big would your donation be to Party funds?'

The Count was puzzled, but it was clear from the look on Streithammer's ugly face that he had some plan or other.

'Fifty sovereigns?' he said, hesitantly opening negotiations.

'Remember it's for a good cause, Count,' Streithammer said. 'It all helps to get rid of that lily-livered leftist red swine in Berlin.'

'Seventy-five?'

'Make it a hundred and you're on.'

'A hundred it is.'

Streithammer beamed. 'Good. I won't forget you, Count, when I take over power. You'll have your pick of the golden geese. Berlin, for example?' he said generously.

'Very good of you, indeed. I really appreciate the honour. But what exactly are you going to do? I mean, Streithammer, where's the private vehicle coming from?'

Streithammer gave the Count his ugly grin and pointed up the road where the black Fiat was now beginning to crawl towards the village. 'There.'

'You mean the OVRA,'

Streithammer nodded. 'I do indeed,' he said.

'What a damn crazy idea,' the Count replied. 'A man after my own heart!'

CHAPTER 3

The South-Tirolean village looked no different than its counterpart across the border in Upper Austria. There were the same shabby white houses with their carved wooden balconies and the tobacco leaves and maize-cobs drying under the eaves. The only difference between this one and the one the fugitives had left several hours before, lay in the communal water tap in the village square. Here it was decorated with the Roman bundle of rods, the symbol of Italian fascism, and a huge, flyblown poster of the *Duce*, his dark pugnacious jaw sticking out threateningly from underneath the gleaming helmet.

The four of them limped slowly down the dusty street towards a line of shabby people. Women covered their heads in kerchiefs and bore baskets of produce, the men in broad black hats and leather breeches, their waistcoats festooned with chains. It was the queue for the morning bus that would take them into town.

The Fiat was parked at the water pump, half way between the four travellers, and the patient queue. The little Italian Humphrey Bogart laboured at the tap to produce water, though like everything else in Mussolini's vaunted 'New Order' it didn't work properly, and only a trickle of brackish, brown liquid came out. It was a facade just like everything else, behind which all decayed and rotted. A country whose

223

core was black with maggots.

A fat priest passed them in a broad shovel hat much like the Count's, prayer-book under his arm.

'*Grass Gott*,' he said, and recognising the big man in the lead, turned around hurriedly and sped back to the little baroque church from which he came. Man of God as he was, he knew trouble when he saw it.

A couple of farm labourers on bicycles, bottles of red wine sticking out of the cheap briefcases clamped behind the saddles, rode through the dust towards them.

'Thick air, Streithammer... *thick air!*' they hissed as they passed, their eyes shooting towards the Fiat and the OVRA man at the pump.

Streithammer seemed not to hear the warning. He shambled on, head bent. The others trailed behind him at the same slow pace. They looked like men who had reached the end of their tether.

Over at the bus queue, the peasants had become aware of the approaching strangers. There was a sudden hush in their conversation. Here and there an old white-moustached peasant started to look at his watch, as if he had decided that the bus wasn't going to come after all, and it would be wiser to go straight back home again. Women covered their baskets. A child started to yell, '*Heil Streit–*' his mother stifling the cry with her hand. The crowd began to drift apart. Suddenly the morning air was hot with tension.

It seemed to take Bogart at the pump a long time to become aware of the strangers bearing down on him. Finally, he straightened and kicked the pump in anger. Looking up, he recognised that something unusual was going on. The pump was uttering a guttural chug-chug sound, but he wasn't paying it any attention. *His kick must have dislodged something*, thought Otto. Bogart rounded on the travellers and fixed them with a dark stare, eyes narrowed into a mean squint. Then as an afterthought he took a ten-lire piece out of his pocket and began to flip it up and down.

'Good grief,' Gore-Browne hissed in spite of his fear, 'it's not Humphrey after all... its George Raft!'

'Be quiet!' the Count hissed angrily, 'I'd just got my quote ready. Now I need a new one!'

After you, then, muttered Streithammer, and ushered Graf von der Weide forward.

Otto could see his compatriot's brain working overtime as they strolled calmly towards the little Italian. *We're bloody close to the lad now. Something needs to happen soon*, he thought.

The Count's hand, clasping the little woman's pistol in his pocket, ran with hot sweat. *George Raft, George Raft,* he intoned to himself. And then he had it! Slowly, he clicked off the safety catch and looked up, straight into the Italian's wide eyes, and said in a terrible American accent:

'So, how tough are you, babe?'

– THE END –

Otto's Adventures continue in...

OTTO AND THE REDS
by LEO KESSLER

Available as e-book & print-on-demand soon.

Printed in Great Britain
by Amazon